I0535958

Table for One Thanks!

D MICHELLE THOMPSON

Table for One, Thanks!
Copyright © 2014 D. Michelle Thompson
All rights reserved
Published 2014.

No part of this publication may be reproduced, distributed, or transmitted in any form or by any means, including photocopying, recording, or other electronic or mechanical methods, without the prior written permission of the publisher, except in the case of brief quotations embodied in critical reviews and certain other noncommercial uses permitted by copyright law. For permission requests, write to the publisher, addressed "Attention: Permissions Coordinator," at the address below.

First published by Faith Books & MORE

ISBN 978-1-939761-14-9

Printed in the United States of America
This book is printed on acid-free paper.

 3255 Lawrenceville-Suwanee Rd. | Suite P250
Suwanee, GA 30024
publishing@faithbooksandmore.com
faithbooksandmore.com

Ordering Information:
Quantity sales. Special discounts are available on quantity purchases by corporations, associations, and others. For details, contact the publisher at the address above.

Orders by U.S. trade bookstores and wholesalers. Please contact Ingram Book Company: Tel: (800) 937-8000; Email: orders@ingrambook.com or visit ipage.ingrambook.com.

Disclaimer
The purpose of this book is to empower, educate, and offer hope. The authors of the book achieved that through their own experiences, expertise, and research. Consequently, this book should only be used as a road map. This book is not intended to be nor is it represented as legal advice. The authors are not liable or responsible, to any person, or entity, for any and all claims, demands, damages, causes of action, suits in equity of whatever kind or nature, caused or alleged to have been caused, directly or indirectly, by the information contained in this book or the authors' past or future negligence or wrongful acts.

ACKNOWLEDGMENTS

Thanks to my brothers in the natural and in the Spirit for helping me stay focused and prepared for the ONE husband God created just for me and me for him.

Thanks to Rev. Watson of Chicagoland Association of Biblical Counseling andDominique Condevaux, LAC of Denver, Colorado for sharing valuable and wise pre-marital information for "Eric & Brinly" and all of us at the table.

Special thanks to all the men I've interviewed over the past few years and to the others who agreed to allow me to share their hearts through the voices of the male characters in this book.

As promised at the Roscoe Chicken & Waffles, Long Beach, California, a special thank you to Mr. Marcel Davis for an eye-opening interview from the "nice guy" looking for Mrs. Right.

Last but not least, special gratitude for my friends, family and Brinly fans who daily inspire me to dine at the table for 1, especially my mother. You are the best!

John 17:21

"I pray that ye all are One, just as You and I are One."

Gloria a Dios! Glory to God!

CONTENTS

Prologue

Eric stood in the hot sun on a dirt road outside Santiago, Chile. He had to shake his head to make sure he was not in the middle of a vision. He was on his second mission trip in four years and had seen visions before, but nothing quite like this one. It was too real.

As the image came closer, Eric knew this was not a vision or dream, but a reality. He stood frozen for a second watching the woman he thought had been gone out of his life for good. There she was, Brinly Marie Daniels, standing near the back of an arriving bus loaded with students visiting for the day. Eric's heart leaped with joy and his mind raced with anticipation. What could he say to the one woman he had regrettably allowed to walk out of his life?

Eric Washington, former college basketball star, now resident tech geek and missionary, was assigned to La Victoria, a school and church outside Santiago, Chile. Apparently, Brinly, too was on a mission trip with one of La Victoria's sister schools.

La Victoria served as the technology resource center for schools up to 500 miles away. Eric had worked with this mission on and off for the past few years when he could get away from work using his vacation time. This was the first year his sites were expanding to include more schools.

Eric was standing outside awaiting his daily busload of visitors when the woman tossing highlighted hair behind her right ear caught him off-guard and immediately drew his attention. To his surprise, he realized she was the one and only Ms. Brinly Marie Daniels, live and in color, right here in Santiago, Chile.

Brinly was Eric's long lost...could he call it love? The girl he'd guarded himself against, keeping her from getting too close to his heart. As Brinly moved toward the front of the bus Eric thought, this must be destiny.

Destiny. Of course. What else could explain the only woman he had ever thought could be the "one" for him standing a few feet away even though they were both 6,000 miles from home?

Eric smiled, remembering their first destined meeting on the way to work on a train in San Francisco, California. Little had Brinly known then that he had spied her out months earlier while visiting her church well before their chance face-to-face meeting on the train. But this time was different. His sight was crystal clear as he saw her in the fullness of who God had created her to be, both in the present and in their future—yes, "their future."

It was time to pursue Brinly to become his wife. Finally, Eric could see himself committing. Finally, he felt he was ready to be the husband he knew Brinly deserved and—whether she admitted it or not—the one she needed.

Eric thought maybe this was his reward from God for all his hard work. He was in month four of his six-month assignment to test the school's new computer lab. He was proud to be ahead of the mission's plan for testing the center. Maybe—just maybe—he could focus on resolving glitches in the system and still pursue Brinly the last two months of his assignment.

Then as he recalled his last encounter with Ms. "pee-or-get-off-the-pot" Brinly Marie Daniels, a thumping fear replaced his joy. A year ago she had pretty much given him an ultimatum to pursue marriage or leave her alone. Eric silently prayed God had been working on her heart—and her mouth.

Brinly's attention centered on counting the children getting off the bus. She didn't notice Eric. Her voice sounded dry and well below the decibels Eric knew she could project. She needed water. Eric hurried to grab a water bottle, and then thought, not good enough for my future wife. He went to the ministry leaders' office where he knew large goblets used for weekend communion services were stored. He poured the water into the goblet. You see, Eric had heard it said you don't wait to start being a husband on your wedding day; you begin as soon as you know the woman you are with is to be your wife.

Eric gently tapped Brinly's shoulder from behind. In his best Spanish, he asked, "Necesitas agua?"

"Si!" She took the glass and drank without turning. She kept her attention on making sure all the kids were ushered inside the school.

Once again, he recalled the "pee-or-get-off-the-pot" speech Brinly had delivered that rainy day outside Fisherman's Wharf, their favorite restaurant. He couldn't help smiling, thinking about her spunk and attitude. It had scared him off from even sending her an email without a purpose. He had wondered why over the past month she had been online at the same times he was. Now he knew.

Eric's thoughts were interrupted when Brinly turned around. "Eric! What are you doing here?"

Laughing, he lifted her in a big hug. The embrace shocked her so the glass dropped from her hand onto the dirty ground along with the rest of her much-needed water. She looked down as if she had lost her best friend.

"It okay, Brinly. We have plenty of water," Eric said, knowing she was still thirsty. "Come on in." He bent to pick up the glass then proudly escorted her into the building.

As the class started for the children, Brinly and Eric kept glancing at each other in disbelief. How could it be they both found themselves at the same place at the same time thousands of miles away from home?

When class was over and the kids were eating snacks, Eric nodded to an open back door and Brinly slipped out with him. He started an awkward conversation, trying to make light of their last interaction, the "pee-or-get-off-the-pot" speech, which, by the way, had been delivered through a taxi window. "You left me in the rain without an umbrella with my heart in my hand," he teased.

Fortunately, Brinly laughed. "You got my point though."

Feeling the need to take advantage of the open door, Eric blurted, "Yes, I did. That's why I've got to tell you right now—uh—Brinly, I want you to know I'm ready. I'm ready to officially court, to pursue you, whatever you want to call it. I'm serious. I'm ready. I'm sorry it took me so long. I just had to get some things together. Actually, I had to let God get some things out of me and together for me. I know that's why we're both here at this very moment." He surprised

Brinly by reaching out to gently cup her face in his hand and graze the tip of her nose with a soft kiss.

The kiss was awkward yet sweet. A kiss only Mr. Eric Washington could pull off with grace and masculinity. Was it the overbearing heat or the unexpected kiss that left her melting inside? Her usually busy mind went blank. She felt numb. Trying to compose herself, she picked her brain for a witty response. She had nada—nothing. No words would come.

Brinly's lack of response scared Eric. He pulled his face away from hers. He felt like a fool. Oh, snap! He had gone way too far too fast. He realized he hadn't even checked her ring finger. She could be engaged for all he knew. Maybe that's why he had seen her online but she hadn't responded. Maybe her man was back home. Maybe—

He reached down and grasped her hands. Blank! Her third finger on her left hand was BLANK. But he still needed to pump the brakes. What is wrong with me, he thought. I let all these feelings overflow because of a coincidence I mistook for destiny. Okay, we're in the same country at the same time. Just enjoy the moment.

But before either could speak, they heard the schoolmaster and ministry leader, Senor Perez, hurrying toward them.

"Perdoname?" they heard him inquiring, "Excuse me?" loudly.

Still lightly holding hands, Eric and Brinly turned to see Mr. Perez scowling. He directed them into his office. As they walked toward him, he called to Brinly's school's bus driver, demanding he return the students to their part of town with a different, more "virtuous" chaperone. Eric was shocked by the schoolmaster's response and could see that Brinly was so insulted.

In the tiny office only big enough for one desk and one chair, the schoolmaster rummaged through his message files while Eric and Brinly stood in silence. After fifteen minutes of silence when the leader glanced at them in disgust every once in a while, he grabbed the dirty goblet as if he were a crime scene investigator that had just found a murder weapon. Under the glass he had apparently located the file he had been looking for.

"Asi, ve aqui conmigo." They looked at the covenant agreement they had both signed in order to go on their current mission trip. The schoolmaster, now serving as sole missionary leader, pointed to line 21, a special rule for singles. "Lee a mi, conjunto"—"Read to me, together."

They both read out loud, but their voices became soft as

they finished the line, "I agree to be fully committed to the call of Christ and will not date or enter into—" Their voices became lower and lower. "—any romantic relationships for the duration of the mission trip."

Oh boy. Mr. Perez had apparently seen Eric's small kiss on Brinly's nose and assumed much more was going on.

Brinly immediately began to explain. Things were not what they looked like, she asserted in her best Spanish. Eric even detected a special lightness he assumed was intended to try to appeal to the schoolmaster's sensitive side. But when she repeated, "—just old friends—" at least three times, he became more angry at Brinly than at the schoolmaster. His "one" obviously didn't think he was her "one." Or was she just a wimp? Either idea turned Eric completely OFF.

Regardless, Brinly's best attempts and charm didn't deter Mr. Perez from throwing up his hands and pointing sharply to both of them. "Una persona tenera revolver a los Estados Unidos pronto!"

Oh no! To show their commitment to upholding the covenant agreement, one of them would have to leave. Mr. Perez opened his brown tattered leather Bible to **Ecclesiastes 5:2, 4-6:**

"Do not be hasty in word or impulsive in thought to bring up a matter in the presence of God. For God is in heaven and you are on the earth; therefore let your words be few. ..When you make a vow to God, do not be late in paying it; for He takes no delight in fools. Pay what you vow! It is better that you should not vow than that you should vow and not pay. Do not let your speech cause you to sin and do not say in the presence of the messenger of God that it was a mistake. Why should God be angry on account of your voice and destroy the work of your hands?"

"It was not what it looked like," Eric pleaded.

At that, Mr. Perez turned to **1 Thessalonians 5:22:**

"Do not give the appearance of evil."

Mr. Perez—or should we call him Minister Pérez—gave Eric and Brinly a full-blown Bible study while they stood in the tiny office. He concluded with how God honors vows and covenant agreements, how we should not enter into covenants lightly, but really plan to walk out the covenants in our lives. Ouch! He was a "letter-of-the-law" type of guy when it came to the Bible. No room for grace.

Eric was so furious. It was just a big misunderstanding, he kept trying to explain in his best Spanglish. He thought Mr. Perez was coming down way too hard. They weren't kissing and they weren't boyfriend and girlfriend—yet. In fact, Eric wondered if that would ever be possible given Brinly's apologetic response to that position. She even offered to be the one to leave.

Then Mr. Perez picked up the glass goblet from his desk and began to shake it to make his points. The schoolmaster went on to further insult Eric, stating that he obviously had issues controlling his flesh. To his surprise, Eric was told to leave immediately.

Eric stared at Mr. Perez, searching for the heart of the man he had grown to love and respect over the years and had served alongside.

Brinly realized she had never seen Eric angry. She kept her head bowed as Eric began to loudly recount all his good works for La Victoria, how he had built the lab over the past few years and on and on. It seemed Mr. Perez was beginning to back down. Then he returned to his seat and asked Eric to be a man of honor and leave the mission assignment immediately. He reminded Eric that he had only two months left anyway while Brinly has four more months to her assignment.

Eric started to leave peaceably. Then he turned to Brinly.

"This is ridiculous. Really, Brinly, you're going to let him put me out and not say anything?"

"Eric, I told him you meant nothing to me," she interjected pitifully. "I mean, it was nothing." Her words were coming out all wrong. But Eric obviously heard, "You meant nothing." Like a flash of lightning, he smacked the goblet out of Mr. Perez's hand and bolted out the makeshift office door so hard the whole shack of a building trembled.

Fortunately, the building didn't shatter. Neither did the sturdy glass goblet. It rolled on the ground without breaking. Brinly immediately picked it up and placed it back on Mr. Perez's desk.

Eric ran out of the school, past his fellow volunteers, past the kids from his mission assignment, past the defined part of the dirt road, till all he saw was open land. He couldn't believe how quickly things had changed since he had seen Brinly earlier in the day. He didn't know what to be angrier about, being falsely accused or Brinly not having his back, and definitely not feeling the same way about him he felt about her. His anger was further fueled by imaginations of being banned from future missions. Out of breath, he stopped running. His bad leg hurt. In his anger, he had forgotten all about it.

He knelt on his good knee and cried out to God.

God, why have you forsaken me?

A gust of wind pushed him off his knee onto his butt on the ground. His right hand brushed something that felt hard. He looked over and picked up the rock near his hand. He got back to his knee, leaned forward and began to write with the stone on the ground.

You are not condemned; you have been redeemed.

His thoughts shifted to the woman in the Bible who had been accused of adultery and how Jesus told her,

"Where are your accusers? Go and sin no more"
(John 8:11).

Eric knew he hadn't sinned intentionally, but in the end, for those few minutes behind the school, the mission covenant had been breached even if only in thought. He remembered his name meant "honorable ruler." His actions the day started out to show honor and ended with him smacking a glass out of his missionary leader's hand. He had to repent, to "go and sin no more," to walk in the fullness of the man of honor God had called him to be.

Introduction

Table for One, Thanks! is the second book in the Table for 1®
series to ignite men and women alike to set the table for one
with their purpose and faith seated at the head of the table.
My heart's desires is for each reader to be empowered to live
a more joyful, purposeful and victorious life at one with God
first and the one another.

In the first book, I described in detail how women struggle
with RICOs (you've got to get the first book) which try to
distract us from achieving this state of oneness with God.

I believe men have similar distractions, but even more
obstacles to living a victorious life, especially while single.
And no, I have not gone soft on the men. I know the enemy
(i.e., Satan, spiritual wickedness in high places, the d-e-v-i-l)
fights men even harder to prevent them from achieving their
God-given purpose and destiny. Why? Because men were
designed to be the head, especially the head of a table for
two. So why not attack the seed-givers, or curse the seed,
before a woman can carry and nurture the seed into life.
Therefore, while women battle RICOs, men, I believe, have
to battle GINAs.

So who or what are GINAs?

GINAs can be:

- **G**littering, gorgeous distractions, made of green or flesh and bone (e.g., too much money or lack of money, and easy-access females)
- **I**gnorance of the great plan God created for you alone (e.g., unbeliever, lack of faith, lack of knowledge of God's Word)
- **N**agging temptations behind every rock and stone (e.g., pride, double-mindedness, lust, addictions of any kind)
- **A**ll persons or situations causing men to moan and groan (e.g., underemployed, undereducated, no father/mentor, past mistakes)

Okay. Went too deep to quick. Let's back up. Of course, men are distracted more easily than women. Why do you think more women can multi-task? Why do you think it takes four-to-five different men to commentate one game between two teams, but it only takes one woman to spew out the celebrity dirt on all of Hollywood in thirty minutes flat? (Oops! My male editors let me get in just this one. Smile!)

Fortunately, for my soul to prosper, I had to learn this lesson up close and personal before I could ever write this book. You see, God told me this book would heal me from every hurt I ever thought was inflicted by a mere man. I first had to stop and look in the mirror and see the hurt I have opened my heart to without being led by God.

The enemy, of course, was mad about this book coming together, so can you guess how many male influences, male co-authors, started this journey versus how many stuck around to see it from concept to actual production? I'll never tell, because that's how my good God has performed His heart surgery on me. But for those who are still here, much love and appreciation.

I said this in the first book and I will say it again—whether you are unmarried or just trying to find "u" in a "union" (marriage), know that God has created you in His image for a purpose, for a destiny that you (as an individual) were designed to fulfill.

While the first book, Table for 1, Please! features the fictional character Brinly and shares the unmarried woman's journey to victorious living, this second book features Eric, Brinly's someday/maybe husband and his journey to living whole, at one with God. The recipe for this book includes a place setting of lessons slightly different for a man. To keep Eric's voice as authentic as possible, male ghostwriters contributed the majority of the thematic journal entries which conclude each chapter.

Finally, but most importantly, this book would not be complete without Biblical references threaded throughout to jumpstart your own quintessential "table for one" with God at the head and your mate by your side.

As I always like to acknowledge, this is a faith-based book. However, even if you do not profess Jesus Christ as your Lord and Savior this book is in your hands at this moment for a divine appointment. Don't miss your date at the table for one.

A special note for the brothers who find themselves reading this book: Please note I have done my research (both on and off the record) with several men and gained input from male ghostwriters to ensure the content in this book is truly from a man's perspective. I hope it inspires you to live a joyful, purposeful, and victorious life and encourages you, in your pursuit of one woman, to pursue the divine "One" first.

For the women reading this book, I have heard the first book brought insights and healing. I am a living testimony that this book will do the same. My heart and prayers for men have truly changed for the better. Okay, I know some of you are like, "Whatever," and others are like, "How?" Here's my top five lessons. I've learned:

1. To be careful what you say to and about a man.
2. To choose silence over castration by tongue.
3. To listen to a man's silence. I promise, you can still hear a lot.
4. To observe actions and not words.
5. To trust God to send the right men for friendship, relationship etc., and the wrong men far, far, far away.

Overall, these lessons allowed my mind to open to the idea of love without fear of failure while my heart remains rooted and guarded by God at the "table for one."

By now, I hope you have read the debut book, Table for 1, Please! If not, I'll review some guidelines. You may have already noticed I am not using the "s" word (i.e., single) too much. I think it's overplayed and gets too much airtime.

I remind you my feelings about the "s" word are not just because it has "sin" at the beginning, and that's what happens to people who are left in that season too long; they get lost in sin. Although that is sometimes true, please recall that my problem with the word comes from my love for Spanish. In Spanish, sin means "without" and the G-L-E on the end (even though there's no extra "e" to make it "glee") means "joy." So when people refer to the "s" word I feel they are saying "without joy." Please know anything created single is created whole, lacking no joy, no good thing.

Whether we are married or not, I believe God deals with us as individuals. In fact, He needs us to lead victorious and virtuous lives as individuals so our partnerships in marriage, business, or ministry have the same result.

Now I hope you will enjoy reading how Eric did it and be inspired or inspire others to do the same. Pray for unmarried men in your life to set their "table for one."

Part I: The Glass

"Single-Minded & Whole"

Especially for my brothers, the journey to living a victorious life as an individual begins by facing the critical fact that you are single with purpose! In the first book, I referred to it as "single and whole" because a lot of times we women seek the exit sign out of singleness for reasons of loneliness or emptiness, as if something is missing. Conversely, I hear my brothers feel marriage gives them a sense of focus, a purpose, and stability, if you will. Often, they will find this in fatherhood even outside of marriage and then seek marriage to close the gap.

But my prayer is for more men to find their purpose, their single-minded focus, during their season of singleness. When I talk to women about the metaphor of the glass at the table I speak more to purpose and how purpose is rooted in the fact that the glass is whole and can hold whatever is placed inside.

As I went further into the metaphor and thought about what men are called to represent, God gave me the metaphor of the glass stem. While I encourage women to be the whole glass not cracked not full of holes, I encourage men to be the single stem of the glass. Notice, there are not two stems, but one, one whole, singular stem which leads to a nice steady, balanced base. This stem and base provide the balance and foundation to the cupped portion of the glass.

Men without a single focus throw the glass off balance. A single man without a single focus will go through jobs, colleges, and women without one single piece of fruit at his table to show for it. But somehow women, out of a need to feel "complete," will be drawn to his table only to sit down in marriage and find themselves starving from lack of food to eat. I mean this metaphorically, of course.

Press Pause. I hear those carnal thoughts. No, I am not perfect. In the past, one of my guiding scriptures when writing off an ex-friend—boyfriend or boo—was always

> *James 1:5: "A double-minded man is unstable in all his ways."*

But the reality, women, is if I were a single and whole woman at the time I would have recognized this man as double-minded from the beginning. I wouldn't have attracted him. Like attracts like. Ouch! Truth hurts. In fact, on the journey to wholeness we will have our very own story of how we became one with God and battled to stay there. I now invite you to walk with Eric through his story from the beginning.

Mission Minded
(Eric at 33)

Eric walked back the exact same way he had run earlier that afternoon. The sun was going down in Santiago, Chile, and thankfully his anger was, too. At least, most of it.

By nightfall, Eric returned to his host family, who had already heard about the "scandal" from other missionaries, to say his good-byes, pack up, and make flight arrangements to go home. He didn't even try to explain himself to them. He'd been redeemed and the truth would one day come to light. The missionary program insurance absorbed all extra fees of changing his flight itinerary. At least he got something out of what he'd paid them for, he thought.

Just before he turned off his computer he heard a Bing on his email. It was Brinly. What now? If she intended to defend him, she was too late. Maybe she was going to refer to his failed courtship request and say, "You should have gotten on the pot a long time ago." Well, maybe this would bring him closure.

He opened it.

Eric,

I pray you read this message in the morning when your

mind has been renewed and your heart refilled with the Holy Spirit. I pray you are restored with the joy of the Lord that no man on earth can steal from you.

Man of God, I've never seen you angry until today. It was so unexpected. I tried to run after you for the first mile, okay the first half mile, okay I ran a little past the schoolyard, and decided you needed to cool off.J (Please smile!)

Anyway, I pray you've run the anger out of you and if not I hope this email cools you as I am praying for the peace of God to rule your every footstep. Everything happened too fast. I'm sorry everything fell on you and I didn't know how to help you. All I can say is, "Walk in peace and NOTHING shall offend you."

Man of God, go home in peace and when you are ready to talk, Skype me. I am here for you.

Praying your safe travels,

Always, Brinly

P.S. I can't wait to start our official "courtship" upon my return. Earlier, I was speechless, for the first time. Only you could do that to me. I guess I had waited so long to hear you say that, I thought I was in a dream or vision for a second, and wanted to savor the moment you became my man of God.

Okay. The first time Eric read the email he did not crack one single smile. Actually, not the second or third time either. He still had some angry feelings and frustration with the lack of support from the woman he thought could be the "one" for him.

But before Eric's twenty-hour flight—with two stops—took off early the next morning, he had memorized the email and fell asleep on the plane reflecting on it over and over again. He awoke to dinner, surprised he had slept through lunch after an earlier stop midday. He bowed his head over his pull-out dinner table saying thanks to God not just for the food, but shockingly to himself, he thanked God for Brinly's note challenging him to live up to being a "man of God."

When he rehearsed the email the fifth time in his head he could hear Brinly's voice saying, "man of God,"—two, no three times—even declaring him to be "her" man of God. Although he couldn't tell by the way she had clammed up in front of the schoolmaster, Eric began to see the importance of someone having your back in the spirit (silence), someone who knows what you pray is more important than what you say.

Eric knew he had to walk in peace and love and not allow Mr. Perez's actions or how he thought Brinly should have reacted to sow bitter seeds into his heart. So after dinner Eric took up the scripture Brinly had referenced, and even the ones Mr. Perez had read. Then he surprised himself by praying not just for his flight (although kind of late considering he was halfway home) or for forgiving Brinly, but also for forgiving the missionary leader, Mr. Perez, the man who made a "right," but not a "righteous" judgment.

Eric nodded in and out of sleep the next few hours. When he awoke he began to pray, this time confidently, about a future with Brinly. And he heard God say, *"Go back to the beginning."*

Over the intercom, he heard, Bing! "We apologize. There will be a lot of turbulence for the remainder of the flight. Remain seated with your seat belts buckled. Also, we are probably looking at a few hours delay."

Thankful no one was seated next to him, Eric stretched his legs across the other seat, all the while keeping his seat belt buckled. Turbulence. That was a good description of his beginning to know God. But what did it have to do with his future?

Everything, he would realize when his plane landed in San Francisco, California, a few hours later. In the meantime, he dreamed about his beginnings.

Mission—Basketball
(Eric at 17 to 22)

Everything is perfect, Eric thought to himself as he dressed for his date with the prettiest girl in school.

- He had a great girlfriend named Jessica.
- He attended one of the country's top prep schools.
- He was poised to achieve his single dream to provide a great life for his mom from playing professional basketball.

Since junior high, dozens of agents and scouts had told Eric he could skip college by playing overseas and going straight into the NBA. The latter made his mom's head shake "no" horrifically every time she heard it said to her son.

Eric's mom, Joanna Stephens, wanted her son to go to college, something she'd missed out on when she left high school early, a pregnant teen, engaged to Eric's father. Eric referred to his dad as a "sperm donor" most of the time. He was a dead-beat father who left Eric's mom in this one bedroom apartment in his family's building and never came back. Eric's single desire was to make up to his mom for all her sacrifices because of his dad leaving them both. So now, he thought, everything was perfect. In a few years his mom's hard times would be a short memory of the past.

So for Eric, even though he held his own with a GPA of 3.5 without any tutors or someone taking exams for him, basketball was his ticket to easy street. At least that's what he thought at the time.

Joanna politely met by phone with the stampede of college scouts and professional agents waiting for Eric to graduate. She even missed a Wednesday night Bible study or two to meet some of them in-person when they made the trip to "help" with Eric's big decision. Eric was strategically omitted from many of those discussions so he could remain eligible for his high school team.

You see, he had three options:

1. Go overseas and play ball for a year then enlist in the professional basketball draft (Mom's least favorite and Eric's favorite).
2. Go to college a year or two then go into the draft (Mom could live with it if Eric promised to finish college online).
3. Go to college four years then play professional basketball (Mom's option; none of the scouts, agents, or coaches for miles around gave Eric this advice).

Joanna Stephens was a tall woman of 5'10" herself and could hold her own. She would drag 6'2" Eric out of bed on Sundays at seven in the morning and make him attend eight o'clock church services before she went to work. Eric would text non-stop on his cell during service, but whenever his mom would look at his phone he would have it touched back to his virtual Bible and make it look like he was reading the scripture. She would just shake her head, knowing he was covering up. Every other Wednesday she was off her second job attending Bible study while Eric was somewhere practicing his game. She didn't care too much for his basketball dreams, but she supported her son's ambitions by letting him miss Wednesday Bible study.

Eric and his mom lived in a two-flat building which his paternal grandparents owned. Although their apartment only had one bedroom, Joanna had creatively turned the dining room into a bedroom for Eric with a nice curtain, a fabric featuring his favorite basketball team. This embarrassed Eric so he rarely invited his friends in. He had them meet him outside. Despite their financial challenges, Eric felt privileged to grow up with family around.

When his grandparents passed away a year apart, his mom's sister, Aunt Loanna, and his cousin Christina moved in on the first floor of the building. Eric's grandfather, Jeremiah Washington, had intended to pass it down to Eric through his mom, but he hadn't paid up all his taxes, and thus his mom lost the building to the state and eventually to a slumlord.

The building was kept up to the bare code minimums. Fortunately, the rent went up only $25 a year.

Thanks to Eric's basketball skills, he knew he could one day buy this building and maybe even the whole block, and call it Washington Street or something to give back to the neighborhood. Maybe he could help other kids who, like him and Christina, were growing up without fathers. Not that he felt he'd missed out on much.

He also couldn't wait to hopefully pay back his girlfriend, Miss Jessica Sanders—if she would still be around—for all she had done in the past year. She attended the ritzy prep school with Eric, and not on scholarship. She was pretty, intelligent, wealthy, classy, the whole package. Also convenient. Jessica drove a red convertible and was willing to scoop Eric from the hood anytime.

Although all those things were great, that wasn't the best thing about Jessica. She was different from the rest of the school. Like the others, her family was well-to-do. Both parents were level-17 in their government jobs and they lived in an eight-bedroom mini-mansion. But she was very down to earth and immediately clicked with Eric. Jessica was the first person who reached out to Eric when he won the basketball scholarship that pulled him out of the Baltimore hood to attend their private Maryland prep school.

All the other preppy students made Eric feel like a fish out of water—except, of course, when he was on the basketball court leading the school to victory after victory.

Eric was the first person, Jessica told him, who related to her for "her," not for her parents' money or her looks. All the guys at school were either too intimidated by her to even approach her or tried really hard to over-impress her. Eric didn't care about all that. Jessica had him at "hello." She was the only person who responded when he asked how to get to his second period class from homeroom.

To their peers' dismay, Jessica and Eric quickly became an official couple. Jessica helped Eric keep up with his studies, especially during basketball season, and even helped him with the long commute between school and home when practice ran late. Meanwhile, Eric knew how to talk to Jessica and make her feel like he listened to her every thought or whim, something she missed and longed for at home, and her girlfriends never talked about anything serious outside of the latest clothing to buy or of course, there was always sex.

Sex—or should we say abstinence—was something else Jessica and Eric had in common. Both had decided to wait. Jessica desired to save sex for her husband and fantasized about a fairytale wedding right after college. She was a devout Christian and believed sex was an act to be entered into only between husband and wife.

While Eric believed in God, his decision was not about his faith. It was about his desire to be nothing like his "sperm donor" father who impregnated his mom in high school. His father proposed to his mom, but never set a date for marriage, and then left before Eric turned two years old. Eric, consumed with his basketball dream, had no desire to be in a situation that could lead to being a father too soon. Therefore, he had no trouble treating Jessica's body as a temple, as she called it.

Jessica and Eric both endured ridicule from their friends about their virginity. Eric was called "Big V" by his teammates because they rightfully guessed he was the only virgin on the team. This was the price his teammates made him pay for making it to varsity while he was still only a sophomore. But the "Big V" label continued through his senior year.

Despite the jokes, Eric thought again, everything is perfect. He was waiting for Jessica to pick him up for a house party on her side of town, just another reason he had to pay Jessica back one day. Although the party was in her neighborhood, she was coming all the way to Eric's so they could attend together.

As Eric buttoned his polo, the phone rang. It was Jessica. She was crying hysterically. Her parents saw a dent in her car and said it must be from her trips through the hoods of

Baltimore. They immediately grounded her from the party that night and forbade her from ever picking up Eric again.

"I don't care what they say, Eric." Jessica's voice sounded muffled as she dried her tears. "I will figure out a way we can still be together. It just won't be tonight. But don't let me ruin your night. Go on and catch a ride with someone and have fun for me, too."

Eric was sorry for Jessica and her car. But at the same time, he was looking forward to the party, the first of the basketball season. Fortunately, he knew a thing or two about girls and women from his matter-of-fact single mother, Joanna. He decided instead of telling her he'd rather go to the party with the big boys, it was best to just tell Jessica he'd stay on the phone with her and they could have a phone date night.

Apparently, he chose right. He got a laugh and an, "Aww, you are the best!" They were talking and planning her escape next weekend so they could have a real date while her parents were traveling when Eric's line beeped. It was a text from his crazy teammate, Allan, one of the few that actually talked to Eric. He wanted to know what time he and Jessica would get to the party. With a few more text exchanges, Eric found himself with a ride to the party.

Jessica didn't miss a beat. "What was all that noise?" she asked.

"Oh, uh, Allan… Looks like he's willing to come all the way over here to get me. Uh, unless..." Eric began to offer up his evening again on the phone.

"No, no, Eric this will be good for you." Jessica was always the optimist that eventually Eric would be accepted by the entire team and the upperclassmen.

Two hours later, Allan and Eric arrived at a house packed with the "Who's who" of Crowley Preparatory—over fifty teens and no adult anywhere on the premises. Great, Eric thought. Little did he know this set the stage for disaster—or should we say, turbulence?

Eric was just excited to be "seen" on the scene. Twelve bedrooms, tennis court, basketball court, and a pool with a pool house. Allan gave Eric the grand tour and casually pointed to the bedrooms that were already occupied. Although it was cold outside, you couldn't tell by the scarves and coats discarded on couches and by the door. The warmth was provided by alcohol served via bottle, can and tube at the entrance of every doorway throughout the house. It was like getting a new cup was the "hall pass" that got you access into the next room. Each room had a music theme of its own.

Eric had a desire for the finer things in life and he knew he would one day get all he desired as he was headed to the professional basketball league. At least, that was what he was told by every scout or coach.

Eric was fine with music and dancing, but felt out of place because he wasn't used to be without Jessica at his side. His first time at a big party, he felt awkward and out of place. Slowly, he moved to a less crowded place in the living room, which happened to be the beer-only side of the room. No types of drugs.

As he started to text Jessica, a soft hand covered his screen and took his phone.

"Hey, stranger."

He looked up to the silhouette of a fine, attractive, slimly-dressed Candace with a full seductive smile. Candace was a video vixen, a "hot" girl, all the guys in school—literally—knew was ripe for the taking, and many had. Eric looked around. Was she talking to him?

Allan, being the jokester, whispered, "She's aiming at you, 'Big V.'"

Candace grabbed Eric and gave him a big groping hug. Eric reached for his phone, but Candace put a beer in his hand and opened the bottle for him. Then she looked up, all smiles, telling him to relax.

"So, Jessica is grounded, huh? A little dent in the car?" Then she said, "Well, we can't have you walking around here all alone."

Eric was very reluctant to even give her the time of day. However, he started to sip his drink. Unbeknownst to him, Candace had laced it with a drug when she opened it for him. His vision began to get blurry. He scanned the room looking for his buddy Allan.

Not feeling any pain, he didn't notice the music go to a slow beat. Candace grabbed his hand. "This is our dance." On their way to the open floor she grabbed two shots from a tray passing around and showed him how to down his quickly. The next thing he knew Candace was on his body like a second layer of skin. Far away from his mind were thoughts of being out of place or anything else, including Jessica. All Eric heard was a soft voice in his ear. "Tonight is all for you, Big V."

Those were the last words he remembered before opening his eyes to his shirt hanging open on the couch in a corner of the room. Immediately, Eric was furious with the thought of losing himself with over-ripe Candace. Without any concern for her feelings, he gasped, "I know we didn't do anything. Please tell me nothing happened with you; especially you."

Candace was taken aback. She wasn't about to tell him he'd refused her advances and pushed her off him. That's how his shirt got ripped as she gripped it for dear life. "You don't know what you're missing, Eric." She'd quickly walked away to hide the tears in her eyes. She couldn't believe she'd been turned down. She resolved in her heart to make him pay. And indeed she did.

Eric didn't bother Jessica with the details of the party. He went to church Sunday morning with his mom, headache and all. Then came Monday.

When Eric left his second class he was pulled into a meeting with his principal, coach and a school counselor. The principal said, "We have invited the school counselor here on behalf of the victim."

Victim? What victim?

The counselor interjected, "Candace Nelson has come to me for counseling after what happened over the weekend. Eric, she says you took advantage of her at an off-campus party."

Candace—over-ripe Candy—actually accused Eric of date rape over the weekend? Now he was in the principal's office where he was asked a series of questions about the party.

The principal added, "We are going to have to call the police, but we wanted to talk to you first about confession and see if you'd like... Well, we are going to have to expel you from school."

Eric lost it. He started to curse. "What the heck! I didn't touch that tr—"

Joanna Stephens walked in the office at just the right moment to calm her son. "Eric, don't say another word. Not another word! Eric, we will get this foolishness settled." Joanna explained her son's rights and that until there was a full investigation there would be no talk of expulsion.

The coach said Eric would be off the team until the investigation was complete.

Eric started to yell, but his mother gave him a look that made him close his mouth and bow his head in shame.

The principal seemed to be intimidated by Eric's mom. "Sorry about this, Mrs. Washington." Then looked down at his file. "Uh, I mean, Ms. Stephens. We know this is a very sensitive matter and the fact your son is only at this school because of his basketball skills, his conduct must always be above the bar. We are going to have to dismiss him from school while this is under investigation."

When they got home Eric tried to explain, but his mother just said, "A mother knows her son. I know you didn't do anything to that Candace girl. But I do know you probably had a drink or two because you didn't have any of your times straight. You better get it straight. I don't have money for a lawyer. That's why you shouldn't even be at that snobby school. They have been waiting for a reason to kick you out, why couldn't you just stay on our side of town? And now I'm missing a half day's pay dealing with this…"

Seeing her son's fear stopped her rant. His basketball dream was at stake. She reached out and stroked his head then hugged him as if he was being taken away to prison the next day.

Eric cried for the first time since he was a little boy. "Mom, I got to play. This is my last season. The big-boy scouts will be here in a few weeks, not just the runners."

Joanna couldn't handle her son's tears. "God is in control," she sobbed. "He will never leave us or forsake us. He will expose the lies." She grabbed some tissue and blotted his face.

Before heading to her second-shift job, she said, "When I get home I want your room cleaned, your homework done, and a full report on what you remember happening at that party.

Oh, and heat up Sunday's leftovers for your dinner tonight."

Sadly, although it was Monday, there were no Sunday leftovers. They were left over from Saturday and Friday. His mom was so exhausted, she didn't even remember.

Yet Eric nodded his head like a zombie. He felt he was in a really bad dream. Date rape? He was a virgin. Just like that Eric's perfect world had cracked. First, Jessica's parents were tripping. Now he was off the basketball team and his single dream was at risk. He didn't even get to see Jessica before he left school. She'd probably heard rumors. He hadn't even told her about Candace's moves on him at the party. He knew they used to be cool and they lived near each other. He didn't want to start a cat fight.

When he decided to text Jessica, he got a strange response: "I'm hanging with Candace. TTYL8R." Eric knew that was the final crack in his perfect world. He was going to lose everything.

By the end of the week he and Jessica had not talked at all and every time he tried to text her she gave a short reply. He didn't want to talk to Jessica about the incident by text and due to her punishment about the car and his school suspension there was no way they could see each other.

The next Wednesday, Eric didn't feel like playing ball in the park with the neighborhood guys. It would just make him more disgusted he couldn't play for the scouts the next week. So he sat home working his other favorite pastime, computers. Like clockwork, his mom came home to change before Bible study. He was just about to figure out a new program when his mother asked, "You coming with me tonight?"

Reluctantly, Eric got up from his computer and went with his mom to church. He looked on in amazement as his mom seemed to experience extreme measures of joy turned to sorrow then joy again all in one service.

He wanted to experience what she was feeling, but he was a little angry with the One his mother was so joyfully praising. All he could think about was his basketball dream on the line because of a lie. How could this God his mother loved so much allow this to happen to him?

Eric bowed his head in shame. When the pastor called people to the altar who needed prayer, he responded. As he made his way forward, his mother rose right behind him. People prayed around him and then he felt a weird, strange peace even though nothing had changed.

The next day after that prayer service, Eric's mom informed

him they had an attorney. Then like a dry-erase marker on a white board, the case was wiped clean. Eric returned to school and played for the final big games of the season in front of scouts from East and West Coast. He even went on to compete against other high school students nationally and was named in a few sports magazines as a player to watch.

Eric recalled the peace he'd felt at the church service that night a few weeks earlier. He thought maybe the feeling was God's assurance that his basketball dream was His plan for him and everything would be perfect. Or so he thought.

A few months before graduation Eric was still undecided whether to go to one of the colleges recruiting him or to go straight overseas to start making money for him and his mom. But he felt like the decision was made for him on the eve of his mom's 35th birthday. Eric arrived home to find his mom with gifts all on the couch and what looked to be the remnants of a nice dinner for two. He'd seen a nice Cadillac Escalade outside and figured since it wasn't the usual SUV rental this must be a slick agent, not a college scout. Eric and his mom agreed he was not to talk to agents at all or this could mess with his eligibility status for college. So taking these cues, Eric headed to his bedroom.

Just as he opened the curtain/door to his dining room/bedroom, out of the bathroom walked a short, beer-bellied man with a slightly receding hairline who smiled and greeted Eric with a loud, "Hello, son, it's so good to finally meet you."

Eric looked down to see the initials of a top East Coast school on the nice polo shirt and realized this wasn't an agent after all. "Uh, nice to meet you," he replied courteously. "And you are?" The college scout wore nice slacks, not from the warehouse, and a watch Eric had spotted in a few men's magazines.

"Coach Riley, Coach Thomas Riley. Your mom and I have been talking about you over the phone for months. I decided to come down and meet you both in person."

Eric knew scouts and schools pursued you but this was a little over the top, unless, of course, the Escalade was for him, then maybe... "Both of us? Looks like you just wanted to meet my mom." Protective Eric flared a little, motioning to the gifts and the remnants of the dinner. His mom was beautiful, and young, and deserved to have a date, but this cool cat was using her to get to him. Or so he thought.

"Hold up, young ginseng. I just like to get to know the parents and the potential players, and your mom told me how you guys have an agreement that no one meets you unless they pass her 'mommy knows best' test."

"Well, did you pass?" asked Eric caustically.

Joanna came into the room. "Cool it now, Eric; and yes, he did pass!"

Eric turned. "You guys make my decision then. I'm going to room." At that moment, as Eric slid through his makeshift divider, he wished he had a door to slam. Then he did what he loved even more than basketball; he escaped on the highways of the Internet, working on his computer.

He was so mad at his mom. How dare she let this scout, coach, whoever he was — short jockey — sit up in their place like this? The guy didn't leave until ten o'clock. Then he was back the next morning to take Joanna to breakfast and drop her off at work. What was her deal? Eric thought.

A few days later, Eric's mom knocked on his makeshift doorframe and asked to come in. Even though he was upset at her he knew it was her birthday. He let her come in.

Although Eric didn't have much money, he was really creative, just like his mom, and maybe even his dad for all he knew. So for his mother's birthday he'd created a video game called Joanna's World. She was the main character and everything about the game represented something or someone important to her. The goal of the game was to get her a million dollars and a mansion.

As Eric showed her how to work the game, she smiled and began to tear up. "Baby, I have raised you since I was a kid myself and I know I wanted us to have better, but I pray I raised you to know I desire more than material things."

Feeling she didn't appreciate his gift, Eric said, "Forget it, Mom. I'll change the game and it will be all about making the angels in heaven sing."

"Stop it!" Joanna shouted. "Now, I know we grew up together, but you will not treat me like your peer. Apologize, right now!"

Eric's head bowed. "Sorry, Mom."

"Look, I need to tell you something," Joanna continued. "Coach Riley is more than just a scout for you."

Eric raised his head to say something, but saw his mother's scowl and immediately put his head back down.

"I don't know how to tell you, honey," she said. Eric could hear the smile in her voice. "We are engaged. At least, we might be. I mean, we met over the phone six months ago when you were going through that mess at school. One of his scouts spoke highly of how he helped players on and off the court. So we spoke and, well, we connected. We started talking on a regular basis, and he's really been a help to me, guiding me through your options. Actually, he's the one who secured your attorney. Then when you came home early Tom, I mean Coach Riley, was surprising me with birthday gifts and a ring." She flashed her left hand.

Eric wanted to cry, but he was too angry. He just stayed quiet out of respect. What could she possibly see in that short old fart? He had to be at least ten years older. Who did he think he was? Maybe the guy was using his mom to get to him.

"I know this is a surprise to you," Joanna said. "It is to me, too. That's why I haven't officially accepted the proposal. Coach Riley and I started counseling at my church by teleconference in a pre-engagement session entitled "Table for 1." The sessions last six-months. At the end I will give my official answer, and I hope I will have one from you as well, one way or another."

"Well, Mom," Eric replied immediately, "while you are making your decision, I've made up my mind. You can get my answer right now." His mom started to interject, then he added, "Not about you, about me. I've decided."

The guy was not going to get to his mom through him. He would go pro as soon as possible. He wouldn't make the biggest money yet, but he'd make enough so his mom would not have to go chasing Mr. Beer-belly.

"Decided what? You are happy for me either way?"

He realized she was still thinking he was talking about her proposal from Coach Riley. Eric shook his head. "No, I've decided I'm going overseas to play professional in the fall."

"What?" she shouted. "Have you lost your mind? I didn't have a chance to go to college. Now you get free scholarships and you choose to flee the country? Baby, can't you see there is definitely no rush for you to go professional? Honey, can't you see God has already provided for me, for you, regardless of basketball, regardless of Tom or anyone else?"

Eric knew she didn't understand how he thought basketball was the answer to everything. At that moment, he didn't want to hear anything about God's provision. He just knew what he had to do. And if his mom was really going to be with Coach Riley he wanted to be as far away from her as he'd always desired to be from his sperm donor. His single purpose was no longer to help his mom by playing professional ball. Now it was to help himself stay as far away from his mom and Coach Riley. Eric even thought maybe he needed to get his own family, just someone all to himself, like the one had once had with his mom. This led him to accept the first overseas offer he received. In the fall, Eric would leave for France.

Then Eric remembered Jessica and how he'd lost her in the Candace mess. So he was totally focused on basketball, not for his mom, not for Jessica, just for himself…and God? He didn't care to know anymore.

By fall, as Eric was heading overseas, his mother and Coach Riley were headed for the altar. He couldn't wait to get away from them. It was sickening. They did everything together. To make matters worse, Eric's mom was moving to the college town where Coach Riley worked so it was like he wouldn't even have a home to come back to.

He stayed in the cramped apartment with his Aunt Loanna and cousin Christina on their couch until his departure date. A week before he left his aunt dragged him to the wedding. After the ceremony, his mom found him—alone thankfully— to say good-bye.

With Eric's first leading lady—his mom—gone, his heart was open to someone new to take that spot, and it wasn't God.

On his way to France, Eric would have an overnight stay in Los Angeles, California. He thought his agent was cheap for selecting a discounted non-direct flight with travel insurance versus a direct without it. But Eric's frustration turned to delight when on the plane to L.A. he met a beautiful model- like little lady named Gina. She reminded Eric of Jessica. She was smart, too, and she was headed west to college. As she passionately talked about her plans to be a doctor one day, Eric wanted to be a flame in her fire. Was it possible to fall in love on a five-hour flight? Is this how his mom felt?

To Eric's surprise, Gina agreed to spend the night with him at his airport hotel and send him off nicely on his way to play ball in France. He thought this was a symbolic way of letting his "Big V" status go just as Jessica had let him go over a rumor. He decided it was time to lose his virginity. He had made it out of high school and would now be making money overseas. But of course, he bought protection in the hotel store. It was a perfect start to his basketball dream. If this woman didn't prove to be the best experience it wouldn't matter. He would never have to see her again. Besides, she told him she knew some French and she could teach him a few things before his flight the next morning. Teach that young lady did. And he even learned a few French words.

In the middle of the night Eric woke up and began to pace. He realized he didn't want to be alone overseas in some country where he didn't know how to speak the language just to prove a point to his mom. He woke Gina and in a flash together they planned how he could start school with her a few hours away in a small town between Los Angeles and San Francisco. Eric told her (who didn't seem too surprised) how he was a top basketball player and any school would want to have him on their team, even at the last minute.

Next morning, Eric called his sports agent. He immediately told Eric where to go, called him stupid and told him how he would blacklist him when he was ready to go professional. Eric just smirked to himself. But the smirking stopped when the agent demanded Eric pay him back for his flight, his Visa, the insurance premium paid on his behalf and all his spending money. At this point, Eric was just glad he hadn't taken any other gifts offered by the agent in the past.

Two weeks later, Eric called his mom. She was too shocked and happy he was in college to care about this Gina girl or what rank the college was. She was so happy she offered to pay the agent back on his behalf.

Eric ignored, the "we" part of her payment plan, it would be both she and his stepfather paying back his debt. He went on to tweak his basketball dream deciding to go pro in three to four years. Just as Eric had predicted to Gina, her school immediately accepted him as a walk-on to their squad. He also received a scholarship after his first quarter. A blessing he took for granted.

Eric liked everything about the campus, everything except the basketball squad. And it wasn't just because they were not a "seed" status team, but the Coach was some Christian fanatic who hosted Bible studies at his house on the weekends, and the team prayed before and after every practice and every game. Eric felt the team needed to work more on memorizing plays and practicing hoops on the court, not scriptures and hooping prayers.

Eric's new basketball dream included playing well enough to bring this team up in the NCAA ranks and get him in the draft by year two. He'd at least get an Associate degree by then. But Gina, his favorite cheerleader, told him he could do it by the end of year one. She was really into basketball, unlike other girls. Eric felt Gina was a part of this new single focus as well. They would have a good life together, especially with her being pre-med and all.

Eric's major was Sports Recreation. He just wanted to do something that allowed him more time to focus on basketball and athletic training. He really liked the Computer Science degree program, but just didn't think he had time to dedicate to it. So Sports Recreation it was, at least for now.

At the end of his first year, Eric had made some strides, but not enough to carry the whole team. In the off-season he and the players were still requested to attend weekend Bible studies at the coach's house. There they were for another Sunday afternoon Bible study, and Eric was called on to pray.

What? No. "I'll pass," Eric said quietly. Then Coach Fanatic—woops, Coach Frank—began to pray.

"Lord, just as your son, Eric, whose name means 'honorable ruler,' has asked to pass on praying, I pray he learns that being a ruler on the court means you sometimes have to pass the ball."

The whole team broke into laughter. Then the coach continued.

"Lord, show all these players your single purpose for them tonight so they may live a victorious life on and off the court."

Just like that, Eric was ready to pounce on the coach after prayer, even if it meant losing his basketball scholarship. He waited for all the players to leave and then approached Coach Frank Stanley.

Coach Frank immediately noting Eric's puffiness. "Son, always seek first to understand. Be slow to anger."

"Coach, what you said wasn't cool." Eric calmed, realizing he didn't mind when Coach Frank called him son.

"What I said got your attention. What I said allowed you and me to talk alone right now, what I've prayed for since you arrived."

Eric huffed, "So now what?"

At 6'6", Coach Frank towered over Eric. "Now you sit down and listen."

Like a little kid, Eric retreated and sat on the ottoman as Coach Frank remained standing.

"When you arrived we were all happy. We knew what a player with your skills could do for this team. But it's not the skills alone we need. We need the right spirit."

"Spirit?" Eric sputtered. "I'm not a cheerleader, I'm a player."

The coach ignored Eric. "Spirit. Son, you must desire more than your own success. Do you even know what it would mean to help a player in practice? How about showing up at the game not just to play your position, but to be ready to help everyone else play their position better? Ultimately, that's our single purpose in life—to play our position, the position God has given us, so well that we help others play their positions better. That's on the court and off the court."

Eric listened like a kicked puppy. "Coach, I'm sorry. I never looked at it like that. I mean, no one has."

Coach Frank acknowledged his humility with a quiet, "Now would you like to pray?"

Eric nodded. He prayed silently at first. But as his confidence in His position in God grew, he closed the prayer aloud. "God, I don't remember when I began to believe in you, but I know I need you if I'm going to be the honorable ruler you've called me to be, not for myself, but to help others. I confess I'm a sinner in need of a Savior. Fill my heart with your Spirit, make me like new so I can live in you. In Jesus' name, Amen." It surprised Eric he had memorized the prayer he had heard Coach Frank lead other teammates through over the past season.

Coach Frank smiled. "I think you feel me."

By the end of the second season Eric was not only the MVP, his team had risen to seed status. Eric was on fire on and off the court, attending weekly Bible studies. He even got Gina to go to church with him on Sunday mornings. Everything was—dare he say—perfect, or almost. Eric even went to visit his mom and Coach Riley for the holidays. But, of course, he brought Gina home as a buffer. That turned out to be a big mistake.

After dinner, Eric's mom and Gina were alone in the kitchen five minutes too long. "What?" Eric heard his mom's voice raised. "Who do you think you are, coming in here and telling me what my son is going to do?"

Eric hurried into the kitchen. "Uh, what's going on?"

"Miss Gina was just telling me about your plans to go into professional basketball next year and how she and you would be living it up in a mansion by this time next year."

Eric tried to laugh it off. "Well, Mom, you knew the plan. I would eventually leave college, and yeah, I haven't asked Gina, because I knew she needed to finish her degree first, but she and I just might be married by next year."

"Where I'm from," Joanna said, "ladies know their place and they don't tell the mother about marrying her son before the son does. But this is a new breed of lady." She looked scornfully at Gina's tights and mini-sweater dress. "Well, definitely a new breed of something."

Coach Riley broke the tension by yelling, "Where's my dessert? I don't care what breed of woman you are. You know there better be dessert." He rubbed his beer-belly affectionately, to Eric's disgust and his mother's delight.

On the flight back to college Eric began to wonder about Gina for the first time in their two-year relationship. She was different, or a "new breed," as his mother stated. He definitely had never mentioned marriage to her, but it was on his mind, sometime later down the road, like his fifth year in the league maybe. It would be better than marrying a groupie...or was she a groupie? No way.

Then his worst nightmare happened to his teammate and friend, Robert. He got his girlfriend pregnant and moved back home. Eric respected his decision and thought at least Robert was a better man than Eric's sperm-donor of a father.

Eric talked to Coach Frank about it. The coach responded in his Jesus-freak fashion with a whole bunch of scriptures for Eric to read. "It's not about getting caught, Eric. It's about getting caught up in things that could eventually destroy you and your purpose."

The first scripture said something about how the "body is a temple, and he who destroys the body, him will God destroy." Eric knew we live under grace and not law. But then he was lead to the scripture that "grace teaches us to say no"

Titus 2:11-14

For the grace of God has appeared that offers salvation to all people. [12] *It teaches us to say "No" to ungodliness and worldly passions, and to live self-controlled, upright and godly lives in this present age, [13] while we wait for the blessed hope — the appearing of the glory of our great God and Savior, Jesus Christ, [14] who gave himself for us to redeem us from all wickedness and to purify for himself a people that are his very own, eager to do what is good.*

Surely God knew his heart. But as he studied the scriptures and prayed more and more at night before Gina came over, he began to feel weird, out of place, like maybe what they were doing was not for him.

One night Eric talked to Gina about testing their relationship. She seemed eager and willing until he dropped the bomb — no more sex. Now, usually this happened to men. But Gina began to act really irritable. For weeks, Eric tried to snuggle and comfort her, but she seemed really upset, especially the night before he going to announce his plans on campus to go into professional basketball. She dressed up and wanted to celebrate, but Eric passed and went to Bible study at Coach Frank's house.

Once Eric didn't have the sex outlet, he had more energy to study, to practice harder, and even wake up earlier. After Bible study, Eric confessed to Coach Frank how since he had given up sex he had so much energy to work off.

Coach Frank laughed. "Focus will come to you more than ever now," he said. The coach volunteered with some kids on the weekends and asked Eric to join him next weekend to burn off the excess energy. Eric immediately agreed.

Eric was excited about the draft, but at the same time he felt a little nervous. He kept thinking about his mom wanting him to finish college and Coach Frank's words, "Play your position."

Was basketball really his Godly position? Was it what God wanted him to do? Volunteering with the kids and Coach Frank the following months helped him see how he really enjoyed basketball more when he was teaching others. Who was he really meant to be; Eric the professional basketball player or Eric the volunteer? Then he heard the words in his head: "Honorable ruler."

Back to the night before his press conference, when he got to his dorm, Gina was already in Eric's bed and had asked his roommate to leave. But Eric, still pondering what it meant to be an "honorable rule," woke Gina and said, "Baby, look, as a man of honor, desiring to treat you as a woman of honor, I have to ask you, please leave. And don't come here anymore unless I've asked you to come over." It came out harder than he wanted it to, but she needed to give him some space.

"Man of honor, my butt!" Gina kissed him on the mouth, the

ear, the neck. When he didn't respond, she got her things and left. Boy, she knew how to make an exit.

As Eric drifted into sleep he wondered, Honorable ruler over what? At least with Gina gone for the night he knew he was ruler of his own body. He chuckled to himself.

In the morning, after the press conference, Eric decided to pay Gina back by surprising her at her dorm. But he was the one surprised.

"Yes, girl, I've tried," he heard through her door. "The boy has 'found Jesus' and now he won't sleep with me!"

Eric wanted to know who his girlfriend was telling about their lack of bedtime stories. She continued, "Now how am I supposed to make sure everything is locked down before he leaves to play pro? I didn't change my major from Pre-Med to French for nothing. I need an insurance plan."

What? Eric was in disbelief. He couldn't believe his ears. His girlfriend was plotting to trap him?

Hearing enough, Eric flung the door open. Not missing a beat, Gina dropped the phone, ran to him and kissed him as if he were her long lost lover. Then she picked up the phone. "Hey, girl, I'll call you later. Eric is here."

Eric pushed her off him. "Insurance plan?"

"Of course," Gina cooed. "I've invested myself—heart, mind, and body."

"You what?"

"I even changed my major for us," Gina said coyly. "I'm no longer pre-med. I'm made French my major. I mean, I've heard the stories about what happens to guys in the league, the groupies and all. I just want to make sure we are solid. On lock, you know?"

Eric was trying to understand. "So sex is our insurance plan?"

Then Gina turned on the "water faucet"—tears streamed down her face, streaking her makeup. "It's just that I don't want to lose you. I know how lonely you were before going away overseas. Surely you wouldn't leave for the league without me."

She'd hit a nerve, referring to how they met. At almost twenty-one, Gina was the only woman besides his mom Eric he had ever opened up to, so naively, he opened his arms and said, "Baby you don't have to worry. You don't have to worry about losing me. Anyway, what if I decide not to go to play ball?"

Gina stopped hugging him. "What? Shut-up, crazy. I mean, whatever. It doesn't matter as long as we have each other." They embraced as Eric's press conference played on the television screen in the background.

A week later, Eric's cousin Christina was in Los Angeles with her boyfriend. She invited Eric to come up and visit. Eric asked Gina to ride with him. As usual, she was way too excited. It was like he'd asked her to marry him. But she knew that besides Eric's mom, in his mind, Christina accepting her would be her seal of approval.

Christina was tall like Eric's mom and could easily have been a model. She was the uppity girl who'd made it out of the wrong side of the tracks, but she took the rough side with her. Her boyfriend, Rico (if you've read Table for 1, Please! you know what to expect) wanted to tear her back down to the wrong side on every occasion he had to take her there. Eric was shocked that Christina and Rico were vacationing together.

When Eric and Gina arrived at his cousin's hotel room the heard Christina and her boyfriend arguing. Eric burst into the room to find Christina, nose bleeding and one eye turning purple, with Rico throwing her up against the mirrored wall.

Eric pulled him away and stepped between them. Rico's next blow hit Eric in the stomach. While Gina ran for security, Eric decked Rico then pulled Christina toward the door. They needed to get out of there.

"No," Christina yelled, pulling away from Eric.

"Come on, Christina!" Eric reached into the closet for Christina's bag, grabbed her by the hand and dragged her out the door. He rushed the ladies into the car he had borrowed from Coach Frank, then sped away.

Rico was soon behind them. Conscious of Rico close behind trying to force them off the road, Eric switched lanes too quickly and hit a guard rail. He felt the car begin to flip then everything went black.

The next thing Eric knew, everything seemed blurry. He heard sirens and screams from Christina and Gina. He couldn't feel his left leg. Just before blacking out again, he heard Gina yelling, "No! No, not his leg."

He woke in a hospital bed, an IV on his right side, his mom, Coach Riley, Coach Frank and Christina gathered around. He left leg hung in a sling in front of him in a big cast.

He looked around. Gina was missing. Gina must have been

hurt, too! "Is Gina okay?"

Everyone just looked at each other as if they didn't know how to answer. Then his mom said, "Honey, don't talk. The doctors will be here in a minute."

"Tell me, mother. I'm not a child. Where's Gina?"

He worried Gina's injuries from the crash had been fatal. But recalling her screams, "No! Not his leg," he knew deep inside, she was not hurt—she had taken off. He had been a fool. He had to admit Gina had been all about the glitter, not about him. He'd known since the day of the phone call, but he didn't want to believe it.

Doctors arrived one by one, at least five. Each one explained the same thing in a different way. Eric had crushed his knee cap and shattered a major bone connected to his ankle. Although he would fully recover, the doctors all agreed, he would never be able to play professional basketball.

Later that night his mom explained he'd undergone three different surgeries on his left leg. Gina had left after the first and not come back. Joanna also delivered the news that he would now be learning to walk with a metal knee.

The next morning, Coach Thomas Riley, his mom's husband,

came by. He and Eric had not shared more than two words since the last holiday. "Son, you okay?"

Eric gazed out the window. "What do you think? And you keep forgetting, I'm not your son."

"Look, man, you know I love your mom, so loving you is autopilot. It's a default switch. A couple years ago, your mom came to be about your former agent, I immediately agreed to pay the debt. Even though you weren't speaking to me. So get used to it. I'm not going anywhere. All your smart-mouthing doesn't scare me." Height or no height, Coach Riley demanded respect. Then his voice softened. "You think I wanted this to happen to you? I was counting on you for box seats and a French interpreter," he added, trying to lighten the mood.

Assuming he was referring to Gina and her change in major, Eric said, "You making fun of my girl leaving me, too?"

"No, no, not at all. Look, I'm just trying to find a way to connect with you. I'm sorry, man, sorry about all of this. But know you have a home with me and your mom. And if you are worried about finishing college you can still get a free ride at the university where I work since, whether you like or not, we are family."

Coach Riley sounded sterner than he ever had as he made his

last point. They stared at each other for a few moments then he left the room.

Eric was grateful to God for sparing his life, but he was confused. What life? Now that professional basketball was a faded dream, what would his life be? Eric had not even thought about school and what he would do next. All he was thinking about was recuperating, learning to walk again, and of course, how he would never trust a woman again.

The next day his hospital room was filled again with his concerned council of four—his mom, her supportive husband, his cousin and Coach Frank. Eric apologized to Coach Frank about wrecking his car, but Coach Frank said, "I'm just glad you are going to be okay. Maybe it happened because you were playing your position as an honorable ruler."

Eric nodded, barely listening. In the lobby he could hear his teammates waiting to come in and show their support. But despite his family, his friends, even his God, Eric felt all alone.

Eric felt like a fool. His stepfather, Coach Riley had paid off his former agent who had bought him an insurance policy in case something like this happened to keep him from playing pro ball. He could have been sitting there with a million dollars in his bank account. But of course, the agent had cancelled the policy when Eric dropped him.

Eric's college roommate came in with Eric's laptop. The nurse powered it up for him. Coach Frank used to keep a blog for all the players to share what they felt about each game, to focus them and to channel their anger or frustrations the right way—through words not fists. It was corny, but Coach Frank knew it was rare for guys to share how they felt without being called soft or something else derogatory.

The team blog was all anonymous, though the teammates could figure out who was who. Eric's name was Lone Wolf. At that moment, he felt more than ever like that lone wolf. But instead of putting his thoughts on the team blog, Eric decided to create his own. He called it "Lone Wolf," and summed up exactly how he felt.

Eric's first entry was, of course, entitled, "The Lone Wolf." Yeah, Eric knew God was in heaven and all he had to do was open his mouth and talk to him, but somehow he felt like words written down sent over the international highway of the Internet had even more power to touch heaven.

The Lone Wolf

I've been blessed with lots of family and friends.
Yet sometimes I feel I spread myself too thin.

Now all alone in spite of the crowd,
I'm turning to you, Lord, to help me with this doubt.
This doubt I have about what it is to be loved.
The love people claim to have for me makes me
feel like the Prodigal Son, 'cause their love doesn't
seem to reach.
I'm an outcast, a lone wolf, serving time inside of
this shell called me.
All my plans have been shattered just like this knee.
God, you said vengeance is mine, so I'm guessing
I'm being punished and this just fits the crime.
I guess I was meant to be a Lone Wolf from the start.
But Lord, if you would, please help me to play this
part.
It is like love is blind and so I live in the dark.
But Lord, must my skin be made of glass to see the
love in my heart?
Or must I be like Job and accept my lot in life?
I am destined to be the Lone Wolf. Help me to stop
putting up a fight. THE LONE WOLF

God didn't answer Eric back with an email, but He certainly answered the cry of the lone wolf in the year to come.

As Eric began to put together a plan that didn't include basketball, he distanced himself from any reminders of his former life (his mom, Gina, teammates) and the accident (his cousin Christina)—everybody except Coach Frank who was like the father he never knew he had been longing for his entire life.

When it was time to be released from the hospital, Eric informed his mother and Coach Riley he would be staying out West and living with Coach Frank while he recuperated. His mother cried, but she acknowledged that Eric was too old to be told what to do. Coach Frank told Eric had had assured Joanna he would get her son back on track.

Coach Frank lived alone. Four years earlier, his wife had divorced him and taken their two daughters. When he prayed for her he always referred to her as his wife, not his ex-wife, so very few people knew they were divorced. He was definitely a man of faith, a faith strong enough to help the Lone Wolf see he was not really alone.

As soon as Eric arrived at Coach Frank's house, the blanket of fatherly comfort was literally pulled from underneath him. The coach ordered him around like a drill sergeant. It was worse than practice. He didn't help Eric get around the house or with his physical therapy. He had to cook for himself and do his own grocery shopping.

Coach Frank knew Eric was trying to avoid his teammates, so if he needed to go anywhere the coach made him call on his old basketball buddies to drive him around. That made it next to impossible for Eric to totally disconnect. Gina was the one person Eric would have loved to call, but she had broken parts of his heart he didn't know existed. He wasn't sure he loved her, but he knew he felt betrayed by her.

Coach Frank also forced Eric's sleeping patterns to change. He had to wake up early for more than just Sunday service. Coach Frank got up listening to Christian music at high decibels at five o'clock every morning and then went for a morning jog at six. By seven, his loud blender would be grinding out his yucky, green juice. No wonder his wife left, Eric thought.

One morning, as Eric got into his handicap shower chair, Eric decided it was time to stand on his own. He prayed, "Lord, could you please help me to stand? Forgive me for every time I've taken for granted being able to leap out of bed. Help me now to stand on my own."

As Eric let go of the chair, in his heart he heard, "You can stand on your own, but you need to remember you are never standing completely alone."

A few days later, Eric took his first shower in months without any chair support. Encouraged, Eric walked downstairs to get some breakfast.

Coach Frank was in the kitchen. Eric shared the testimony about his progress. Coach Frank who gave him a pound on his back. The coach was proud, but as always, he kept pushing for more. "So now are you ready to play your position?"

"What? You heard the docs. I'm not going to play professional ball."

"Eric, your whole life basketball has been your dream. Being a point guard is not the only position you are called to play in life."

"Yeah, I thought about computers, but you know I'm sick of being a student. The accident has made me lose time. And it's not like I have a scholarship anymore. It would all be on student loans."

"Eric, your time is not God's time." Coach Frank never let up.

Eric started his "Lone Wolf" cry: "I hear you, Coach, but I've made up my mind, I don't want to be a student anymore. It's time for me to start working. I called my academic counselor and asked about the Computer Science program, but the dude said it would take another two years, and like I said before, I've already lost too much time. Besides, I never thought I was going to need a four-year degree."

Coach Frank began his "State-of-the-Man" address: "Look, Eric, I told you before, time as you quantify it is not important. You'll see one day. God redeems the time. Time is in His hands. I'm just glad at least you called the counselor to investigate your options."

"So," Eric concluded, "I hope you'll support me when I tell you I've decided to finish up my Sports Recreation degree this year and then I'm done. But there's just one thing."

"Okay, young man, what?" Coach Frank asked.

"Well, I don't want to move back to campus. I don't like the stares about what happened and well, I just don't like being around a lot of people anymore."

"You can stay on one condition." Coach Frank always had a condition.

"Yes, sir?" Eric was ready to agree to almost anything.

"You got to get up and meet God with me."

That irked Eric to no end. But he really wanted to be done with campus life, Gina and stares from knowing students, so he replied, "Can we do six?"

Coach Frank replied, "Meet me in the living room at five, starting tomorrow."

"But classes don't start for another month," Eric insisted.

"Yeah, boy, but you're living here now. Rent free, I might add." Coach Frank smiled and hit the blender on his green juice. Eric took a bite of his toast. At least he wouldn't have to drink that goop.

The next year went by fast and meeting God with Coach Frank wasn't so bad. Eric moved from just asking God into his life on occasion to asking God to reside in him daily. After he would meet God with Coach Frank, Eric would type on his blog before getting ready for class. A few times he was almost late because of his strong connection to God and writing after prayer.

One morning he found himself writing God's rebuttal to his Lone Wolf cry.

> *The Lone Wolf is Never Truly Alone*
> *Lone wolf, you were never all alone.*
> *In a crowd or by yourself, you are being shaped for*
> *My throne.*
> *The love you've been seeking rests inside of Me.*
> *I just need you by your lonesome to find my love is*
> *the key.*
> *This key unlocks your destiny from the start,*
> *To direct your single mind, body, and heart.*

Ding. *Eric heard the pilot make another quick announcement and returned to sleep on his long flight home to San Francisco.*

Part II: The Knife

"Cut the Substitutes"

After victorious individuals recognize their purpose, they must pick up the knife at their spiritual table and begin to cut out all the substitutes and distractions preventing them from walking in single-minded focus that honors God first and foremost. When I speak, write and teach, my single-minded goal is that you find more joy, purpose and victory at the table for one.

At this table for one, the knife is the weapon of choice because it is the only thing that can defend you in your weakest moments.

As I interviewed men who had taken a seat at the table, thought about the table, or driven past the table, there was one unifying element—MONEY—the pursuit of it or the lack of it.

For many young men, money is a substitute for God at the table for one. Initially, I was going to say women were the main substitute, but often women are merely a byproduct of money. For example, financially successful men tend to attract women without intentionally trying while less wealthy brethren tend to invest time pursuing and collecting women as if increasing their bank account balances. Woops—some actually did.

What about sex? That was up there, too, but that was not

unique to women. In fact, not to blame women, but to show the male side of the table. It was reaffirmed that women hold the power of influence when it comes to sex. Men shared how they never explored abstinence or holiness until they met "the one." Other men shared how when they did decide to limit or abstain from sex, church was the worst place to be when trying to avoid temptation. One guy stated, "Women are so happy to see a man in church." Between low cleavage, tramp stamps (lower back tattoos) and overt requests for house calls non-prayer related, what's a guy to do. Smile! Of course, this can work on the flip side of the table so back to money.

Since sex substitutes worked on both sides of the table, I found money played a bigger role than women did as it relates to substitutes. It really all goes back to the beginning. Let's peek at Genesis real quick. After the fall of Adam and Eve men were cursed to work and sweat while women were cursed with labor pain. Interestingly enough, most men and women substitutes have to do with money/career, children, or the pursuit thereof.

Of course, men and women alike have used each other as substitutes to some degree, like ATMs, making withdrawals from them and leaving deposits of broken hearts, children without two parents in the household, STDs and a host of other soul-ties. We don't see it like that or don't want to see it like that. Knowingly or not, we "practice" divorce not for marriage, switching out people for fit emotionally, physically or both.

For example, I know of a guy who has one girlfriend who does his laundry, another who provides him with season football tickets, and still another who spends the night. He doesn't think he has substitutes; it just takes several different women to fulfill his needs in life. On the other side, we have a young lady with one man to pay her bills, another to fix her car, and another who's good with pipe cleaning. I'm not judging; I'm just saying it works both ways. But we all need to close our eyes, repent to God and ask him to remove anything or any person He does not desire to be in our lives. We all need to cut the substitutes and wait on God.

Spiritually speaking, the knife is our sword—the Bible—our weapon, the Word of God. When the Word is in our hearts it will guide our words, thoughts, actions and reactions. At the table for one, the knife gives us the ability to cut the substitutes and wait.

Let me repeat this another way. Anything or anyone that occupies space in your life without a divine purpose is a substitute. It can be a relationship not orchestrated by God that fills your heart with emotions you are not prepared to handle.

For the married man or single father substitutes often take the form through the divine (wives or children), but are manipulated to tear them away from holding onto the "you" God created you to be, regardless of your social status.

Lastly, substitutes can be career, pride, misplaced loyalty to old friends, bad habits or simply misplaced affections that fill your time, thoughts or take your money, but do nothing to increase the joy, purpose and victory you can have at the table for one.

We all have substitutes of some sort, and they are not easy to cut away. But it gets easier when you realize it is a war, not a small battle you're willing to lose.

Something I've started to do is regular confessions and visualizations. Now, before you think I'm getting all hocus pocus, wait! What I'm saying is to help you cut those nagging substitutes out of your life, please don't reject before understanding. Smile! I intentionally confess and ask God to remove substitutes on a regular basis. Every time I am tempted to pick up a substitute (temptation will come but God has given us power to overcome), I picture myself in the palm of God's hand, in His will, under His thumb of protection. And then I ask myself, is this substitute thing or person worth leaving God's hand of protection?

Please take a pause of silence. Confess, visualize, and then continue.

Still not sure how to judge what is or is not a substitute? Read God's word. We will explore this more in Part II: The Fork.

As we'll see, Eric needs to use his knife to stay true to the meaning of his name and purpose, "honorable ruler."

On the plane, Eric nodded awake to hear the announcement— only three more hours till he would be home and back to life as normal. Or was it time to begin again? He closed his eyes again, remembering what it was like to begin again after letting go of his basketball dream.

Living on Purpose. No Substitutes
(Eric at 23-26)

Exactly a year after Eric decided to go back to college, he completed a degree in Sports Recreation. It was the quickest way he could put college behind him. Along the way, his computer affinity led to online porn.

He was caught once by Coach Frank, and it was like a metal curtain came down. Coach started restricting him to use the computer only for study sitting at the dining room table. The coach explained to Eric how this was like a drug addiction and shared with him the scientific, not just the spiritual, reasons Eric was setting himself up for failure.

By graduation Eric, with the help of the Holy Spirit, had kicked his habit. He appreciated Coach Frank for his encouragement and help. That's why he listened when Coach advised him to obey his mom and walk at graduation.

Eric had continued to keep his distance from his mom post marrying Coach Riley. But he realized, as his mother's only child, this was her only chance to participate in a college graduation. He shook his head, remembering how his mom had given up college for him. Yeah, Coach Frank was right; he had to celebrate his graduation.

Eric even invited his cousin Christina, despite not talking to her since the accident. He had avoided her because she kept apologizing all the time. He couldn't get her to understand that though his basketball dream was over, his life was not.

The small graduation dinner party at Coach Frank's would have ended uneventfully except that Eric's mom announced she and Coach Riley were with child. What? That was the nail in the coffin of their relationship. It confirmed his need to start his own life and keep it on the West Coast away from his mom's new family on the East Coast. Eric the lone wolf (never truly alone with God) took the first job he found in San Diego, California at a recreation center.

Eric still wasn't ready to fully embrace God's love, but he was ready to be single-minded—he just needed to invite God into his mind.

Eric's single mind was made up to have God at the head of his table, but he sometimes got distracted from the table. His job with the Department of Recreation for San Diego was very cool, though it didn't pay enough for him to live in the expensive city on his own. So he shared a house with three guys he found online through the city employees' intranet site.

His roommates were an interesting mix of Country, Gospel

and Rock & Roll. Troy, the oldest at thirty-five, was a big-time "player," and none of his game was on the field or the court. Troy was a police officer and owner of the house. He rented out rooms to make extra money. He also figured it was a good way to make sure his women wouldn't set up shop in his house. At least some of them. He found out some weren't that bothered by the other men. Their biggest concern was that he owned a house. So Troy started telling them he was renting from one of the other guys.

Eric's other two roommates where seminary students at a nearby Bible college. Other than attending the same college they were very different. First, there was Lloyd. Everybody referred to him as the forty-year-old virgin. Although he was only twenty-two, after one conversation, everyone knew he would still be that at forty. He was the son of two missionaries and a devout Christian, mild-mannered, and he kept to himself. Then there was his colleague, Adam, the exact opposite. He was actually an Atheist going to a Bible college to prove Christians wrong. Well, at least at first. Then he became a Christian. After that he spent his weekends doing street evangelism on every corner he could find. He had a harem of women that followed him around, but he claimed they were just attracted to his "anointing."

All the guys agreed on one thing—no sharing the food. That meant two refrigerators and two freezers. When they threw a barbecue you would find Troy playing guitar for his friends in the basement, Lloyd and his crew playing chess on the patio, Adam holding a Wii tournament in the living room, and Eric, the master chef, at the grill. The only time he got frustrated was when some guy recognized him and wanted to play a pick-up game of basketball.

While home life was always interesting, Eric really wished he made more money, and sometimes wished he were still in college. He switched jobs three times in the first two years, but still didn't make the kind of money he needed to live on his own.

His personal life was null and void. He could barely afford to eat, much less feed anybody else. He was still paying for that last year of college out of his own pocket since he'd lost his basketball scholarship. So it wasn't Eric's call to celibacy as much as his call to save money that left him alone in the house most Friday and Saturday nights.

Furthermore, he really didn't want to risk putting his heart on the line again for a woman. He used his weekend nights to work on his blog without a roommate walking into his room unannounced. Eric also still liked anything computer-related, so this was his private time to be the closet nerd he really was at heart. Sometimes in these alone times he would find himself navigating to a porn site and would immediately shut his computer off and flee from temptation. Then Eric would think about designing software, and of course, he still enjoyed creating his own video games.

One Sunday morning in the shower he thought about the day he prayed to God that simple prayer to stand on his own two feet and how God answered, just like that. Then he went to his blog and realized he hadn't asked God for anything in a long time. It felt weird, like God had already been so good to allow him to walk again, he didn't want to bother him.

Eric wanted to make more money, but maybe he needed to ask God how to make it. He didn't want to ask because he was ashamed he had never tithed, and his offerings were sparse at best. Why would God bless him? His thoughts went from walking again to running out of college. Maybe God had wanted him stay in school two more years for a different degree. Eric shook his head thinking what will be, will be. Then his cell phone went off.

It was Coach Frank. They hadn't spoken in months.

"Hey, Eric, how's everything going on your new job?"

"It's a job. I make a little more, but didn't realize the taxes..." Eric realized he was complaining and tried to turn it into a praise report. "But I'm blessed to have a job. So many people graduate and don't get a job in their fields for years."

"Well, this may sound crazy," Coach Frank began. "I know you've only been on your current job four months, but I want to invite you to come back to campus."

"Look, I remember what you said about that Computer Science degree," Eric said. "I've thought about it, too, but there is no way."

"Wait, son. Hold your horses. Just come for the career fair being hosted by the department of Computer Science. All the companies from Silicon Valley will be down for the day. I've got a friend who can get you on the interview schedule. You interested?"

"Of course, but my degree is not in the field…"

Coach Frank countered with the Word. "'With God,' what?"

"All things are possible." Eric halfheartedly concluded the Bible reference from Philippians.

"What?" Coach Frank challenged Eric to repeat it.

"All Things Are Possible!" Eric shouted into the phone like he was back in the locker room before the big game.

"Amen. See you next Friday, 10am." Coach Frank hung up abruptly.

Eric put down the phone and did something he had not done since before the accident; he got on his knees—despite knowing the struggle it would be to stand up—at the foot of his bed. He repented for not tithing and asked God to enlarge his territory, vowing to give whenever he had the opportunity.

The morning of the career fair, he prayed before heading to his appointment. His roommates wished him well. Lloyd even asked that they pray together before Eric left.

Eric needed those prayers. Arriving on campus, the first person Eric saw was Miss Gina. She was parked right outside the Career Service Center as if she owned it. "Eric," she said timidly. When he walked away, she called loudly. "Eric!"

His stopped and turned toward her, but with a resolved confidence unlike the man she'd known before. "Eric, you are walking pretty good. You look great! I heard from Coach Frank you might be here."

"Look, Gina, I can walk, but I can't play pro ball. Oh, and that walk you see is with a metal support in my knee, remember?" Without giving her a chance to respond, he continued. "Oh, you wouldn't know that, would you? You left before that."

All the anger and bitterness he had held toward Gina gave

his words a hard edge. He'd thought for years he knew the man inside him, but now he realized the pain in his heart.

Gina put her head down. That's when Eric noticed how she was dressed. Gone were her low, cleavage-displaying tank top and short jacket. She wore a simple sundress with cap sleeves and a gathered waistline that flared below her knees. She looked back to Eric with tears in her eyes. "Okay, I deserve that. I'll own that. But I—I gave my life to Christ. I go to church for myself now, not for a relationship with you. I actually just wanted to apologize. You deserved—deserve—better than what I could offer you. I was just a messed up little girl who never had a dad and saw my mom use men to pay bills my whole life."

Funny, Eric realized he had never even wondered where Gina's father was, maybe because he didn't care about his own.

"But with God," she continued, "I now have a new mind and it's made up again to be a doctor. So I'm finishing med school next year. In a weird way, it's all thanks to you."

She tip-toed up to him and kissed him on the cheek. Then she swiped at a tear and walked away.

Eric looked at the girl he'd once thought could go the distance with him and called after her. "Thanks, Gina. I forgive you. Really, I do. Thanks." Then he went on to his interview.

He had come back to campus for a new open door, but it was fitting God would completely close an old one. He said a quick prayer, asking God to use Gina in the medical field. He also asked for complete healing for both their hearts for whatever God had for them next as victorious individuals.

During the interview Eric was thankful he had spent the better half of the last four years interviewing. He was ready for the Silicon Valley interview squad. Two hours later, he left with an offer to be a sales rep and a chance to work his way into the software engineering department. There was just one catch. He had to go back to school. The company would pay for graduate degrees, but he would need a Bachelor's in Computer Science.

Eric felt defeated in one way, but elated in another. Walking to his car, he saw Gina again. This time he approached her. She behaved shyly, which seemed to Eric like a first. She waved and said, "Bye, Eric. Best to you."

Eric leaned down and hugged her. "You too, doc. Best to you, too!"

With Eric's soft pat on her back, Gina breathed a sigh of

relief as if she felt truly forgiven. Eric didn't want to be her new best friend forever, but he did wish her well. After all, he had to play his position and that meant helping others play theirs. Forgiveness is something we all need at one time or another.

Once in the car, Eric's mind flooded with thoughts of his new career. Software development was not just a dream, it was a calling for how God was going to use him. But for what? He felt frustrated this calling had not been more apparent years earlier when he was recuperating from the accident, when he'd raced to get any degree versus the one God had called him to since a young child. He had taken the easy way out. But God reminded him, "I will use everything about you for My glory."

Before heading back to San Diego, Eric called Coach Frank and invited himself to dinner, which of course, was no problem to Coach Frank. He asked the coach if he should go back to school and work at the same time. Coach Frank advised him to start the job first to see if this was truly the company he wanted to work for long-term.

"Eric, it's a big commitment and investment to go back to school." All-knowing Coach Frank confirmed Eric's own thoughts.

"You are right, coach; you are right. I'm glad when I lost basketball I didn't lose my coach." Eric smiled. That was probably the first time he'd acknowledged something positive in his life not related to playing professional basketball.

"Son, I'm just glad you knew there was more to life than basketball."

Eric took Coach Frank's advice. He quit his four-month-old job at the Community Center and took the job at IP Designs, Inc. Although this new job doubled his salary (which wasn't hard to do) and gave him a bonus, he didn't want to move into the Bay area closer to work immediately. It was quite pricey there, and he wanted to first prove to himself that he could afford it. And as Coach Frank had said, he wanted to make sure he liked his new career choice.

After a few months, Eric was missing the kids from his former job, so he volunteered at community centers on weekends when he wasn't traveling. He liked selling software, but he knew he'd love creating it even more. Eric was a geek at heart, and with basketball out of the way, he didn't care who knew it.

He wanted to share the news with his cousin Christina. He hadn't spoken to her since his graduation. Christina hadn't reached out to him either. So Eric called his mom and asked for Christina's newest number.

As the phone rang, Eric pondered what to say. *Cuz, I'm glad my knee got shattered, because then God could put my heart back together?*

"Hello?" Christina sounded confused. She probably didn't recognize the area code and had no idea who was calling.

"What's up? It's your favorite cousin/brother." With the recent distance between them, Eric thought he'd better remind her of what she used to call him when they were growing up.

"Eric! Hey, uh how are you?" She sounded flustered. "Uh, how is everything?"

Eric decided to cut right to the chase. "Christina, you know it wasn't your fault right?"

"But in so many ways it was. Eric, it was." All the pain of the past four years filled her voice.

"Listen, Christina. God has a way of taking everything—the good and the bad—and working it out for our good. Trust me when I say it's all good now." Speaking this testimony caused Eric to believe it even more.

She said, "Eric, thanks. I needed this call. I wanted to reach out to you, but didn't know how."

"Christina, I had to be alone for a while to lick my wounds and to figure out what was next in my life. That's why I called."

"Really, what's up?" She sounded perkier.

"Well, I'm thinking about going back to school to get my degree in Compu—"

"About time you owned up to being a nerd," she interrupted, laughing, before he even had a chance to finish the sentence.

"Okay, so don't you think I'm crazy? I'm mean, it's like I've taken two years forward in the wrong direction and now I'm taking two years back as it's going to take me two more years to get this second degree."

"Weren't you the one who just said God uses everything? So he will use those two years working with kids and he will use this degree."

Eric smiled at his cousin's ability to throw his own words—and God's promise to him earlier that day—right back at him.

"Okay, okay," he laughed, "but do me a favor."

"Sure, cousin. Anything."

"Come out to my mom's and Coach Riley's for the holidays with me."

"Eric, cut the substitutes. It's been almost seven years. It's time for you to stop putting people buffers between you and your new family." It sounded to Eric as if Christina had been talking to his mom a lot instead of talking to him.

"No, no, that's not it. I just wanted you to be there when I tell my mom I'm going back for a second degree," he lied.

"Eric, we haven't talked in a while, but for real, man up and get to know that person called your stepfather. He's actually a good guy."

"I know, but it's weird. It was just me and Mom for so long."

"That was the past. Live in the present. And don't worry about the future."

"Alright, cousin. I'll think about it. And, uh, when did you become the big counselor?" Eric didn't want to rub in all her Ricos, but she sure sounded different.

"Yeah, I know, right? Actually I was tired of the cycle and went to counseling, a place your mom and stepfather recommended called Table for One Biblical Counseling.

They help singles and couples who just want to make sure they're ready for a healthy and whole relationship." She sounded like a television commercial. And she sounded on the right track for once—personally and professionally.

"Good for you, Chrissy," he said warmly. "But sounds too deep for me. I'm just trying to go back to school and do what I was called to do."

"Laugh now!" she teased. "You'll be calling me one day soon asking for the number. Your mom told me you haven't talked about dating anybody since that Gina girl."

Now Christina was probing into his love life. "Okay, foul! Not cool. We haven't really talked in years, and now you're all up in my bizness." He was only half-teasing. "Yeah, that's true, but I talked to Gina today we're in a good pla—"

She'd interrupted again. "I know you are not even thinking about letting that gold digging tri—"

He cut her short. "Good to know the old Chrissy is still alive and well. No, I meant we are in a good place, but separately. I'm letting go. We all should, you know, Chrissy—let go, I mean. Don't look at me and remember where you were. Look at me and see your cousin/brother, ride-or-die-sidekicks for life."

Christina began to cry. "Having my back almost got you killed, and it's hard to deal with that. My bad choices in men almost cost me the only man that ever truly loved me." Christina's dad, like Eric's, had left the scene before she was three years old.

"Christina, you sound like you are making better choices, so start by choosing to forgive yourself. In fact, I think we need some cousin time. You should plan a trip here before the holidays."

"Well," Christina muttered, "Actually, I'm in the Bay area at least two days a quarter for meetings with work. Maybe we can grab dinner one night, if you aren't too busy with the new job."

Eric replied, "Sounds like a plan." Had he really been that unapproachable since his accident? He'd left everyone he loved most alienated from him.

Christina said, "Thanks, Eric. Thanks for calling. I really needed to talk to you."

"Me too, cousin/sis. Me, too."

A few months later Eric headed east for home—well, not his real home—Coach Riley and his mom's home. It was a cute little white Tudor house with a white picket fence in a college town where everybody knows your name and your family. And it came with an adorable baby brother sleeping in the bedroom next to his.

Coach Riley had a few of his players at the house for Christmas Eve dinner. They were the guys that didn't have anywhere to eat for the holiday. A few of them had followed Eric's short-lived basketball career and told him they were sorry about his injury.

An apologetic Coach Riley tried to usher his players to the basement to avoid an awkward moment for his stepson. But to his surprise, Eric followed them to the basement and took the opportunity to share his testimony with the young guys. He encouraged them to have a Plan B, and even their Plan A should be for the right reasons—more than just money.

Later that evening, Coach Riley and Eric found themselves alone while Eric's mom rushed to finish errands and last minute Christmas shopping. Typically, when they talked at all they talked sports and that was about it. But that night Coach Riley asked Eric, "Why are you staying on the West Coast? Is it because of me and your mom and brother?"

"Well, actually..." Eric looked down a few moments, then met the man eye to eye. "Honestly, it used to be. But now it's my career. I just landed a job in Silicon Valley and this is what I was born to do. I just have to stay focused and go after a second degree." Eric had accidentally slipped the news to Coach Riley before his mother.

"Second degree? Nice! I'm glad it's not about us anymore. But you need to know your mother thought it was because you were looking for your father. She thought you wanted to find him and forget about her."

Coach Riley looked sad. His dad? Funny, it had never occurred to Eric to look for his sperm donor.

Riley continued, "She and I want you to know this is your home, and we will always be your family."

"Coach Riley," Eric sighed, "I'm sorry I've been a punk. I'm trying to grow up now. It just hasn't been... Anyway, uh, I get it—we're all family. And make sure my mom knows, there is one thing I don't desire—to meet my biological father. She never has to worry about that..." Eric thought about God's words: Everything about you. "...unless God shows me different."

He stood and walked upstairs, not wanting to go there with the man he barely knew.

Eric awoke the next morning to a college catalog slipped under his door. Inside, his stepfather had stuck a note that said, "Your mom and I support your new career." Eric flipped through the catalog, thinking, they're just trying to get me back on the East Coast. Then he saw an online degree program in Computer Science circled in red.

He had to admit to himself that Coach Riley was a man of action, not just talk. He was still willing to let Eric go to his college as part of his family plan—tuition free—leaving Eric with no money concerns for his second degree.

Eric felt like shouting, yet was humbled to silence. He'd greeted the day without greeting the one who had been his Father so many years before Coach Frank, before his stepfather, Coach Riley. Eric got on his knees and began to pray.

At breakfast, Eric shocked his mother by hugging Coach Riley first then kissing her on the cheek. He even—for the first time—offered to feed his baby brother, Samuel, so his mom could finish her breakfast. He actually thought he heard his mother praying in another language under her breath as she said, "Pass the orange juice, please!"

When the family posed for a Christmas picture by the tree, Eric squeezed in with them instead of standing like a lone wolf on the opposite side of the tree from the others. He even promised himself to buy Coach Riley a nice gift next year, not the usual gift card to an electronics store. Too late for this year.

Back at home, Eric called Christina and thanked her for her advice to cut the substitutes when it came to dealing with his stepfather.

"Eric, did you really just call Coach Riley your stepfather?" Christina asked, a smile in her voice.

"Yeah, right," Eric admitted. "It only took me six or seven years."

"God forbid any woman try to win you heart," Christina joked. "It would take at least ten years."

"Try fifteen. I'm focused on my purpose and calling," Eric responded with serious determination.

His phone clicked. "Hold on Christina. I've got another call."

Clicking over, Eric heard Stacey's voice, the nice young lady at church who offered to take him to a black-tie gala event. He told her he would call her back.

"Hey Christina, you there?" Eric asked.

"Yep, still here, ladies man."

"Naw, you got it wrong. That was a nice lady from church," Eric began to explain.

"Whatever. I've heard church is a player's amusement park." Christina started to recant stories she had heard.

"Come 'on, Chrissy. You know I'm a player only on the basketball court."

There was a pregnant pause, both of them thinking about his botched knee and NBA career. But Eric quickly interjected a laugh to lighten the air. "You need to get out here and go to church with me. It's the women playing the games big time, especially in the heart of San Francisco. A bro can't pass the offering plate without getting a number written on the back of an envelope."

"What, are you an Usher?" Christina said with thorough laughter.

"Nah, that's just it. I'm only a benchwarmer in the pews and I'm getting that much action. I talked to my old roommates Lloyd and Adam who are going into ministry and they said it is worse for them. Always someone needing a prayer or a shut-in visit. Let's face it. The worst place for a brother trying to be celibate and live 'holy' these days is the church. Everywhere, beautiful single women, all colors, shapes and sizes. The boldest ones get your address and pop over with a cake or pie on your birthday. But to be clear, the girl that called is not like that. Stacey is all business. She a local politician and needs an escort for a black-tie event. She knows I need to network for my new sales job so we got a good deal." Eric hoped he sounded matter-of-fact.

"Well, what about the girl your mom told me you brought home one time, Barisia?"

"Okay. That tears it. You and Mom talk too much! Besides, Barisia was too hot to handle. I still hang with her sometimes, but I keep it to dinner and a movie 'cause I know she is trying to get married and I'm not!"

"Of course, you don't want to get married," Christina challenged. "You've got three wives—Black-tie Stacey, Dinner and a Movie Barisia, and your spiritual sister you call homey when you guys talk to the wee hours in the morning. Her name is Lynette, right?"

Eric shook his head, "Women! Y'all love to take notes and throw stuff in a man's face. Watch it, cuz! We just started talking again." Though he was joking, Eric wondered, lining up all three women in his mind.

"Okay, but you know I got a point, Mr. 'I'm-not-a-player.' I think you could put Mattel and Parker Brothers out of business."

Eric was enjoying the old brother/sister verbal exchanges. "Trust me. I know it sounds a bit much all at once, but spaced out, they all play their positions for what I need at that point in time." He spouted that out before he realized what he had said.

They both burst into laughter at the same time for the first time since they were kids.

"Eric, sounds like you got substitutes from your past hindering your present," Christina analyzed.

"What are you talking about? I told you I'm over being Mama's boy, and I embraced my stepdad and baby brother."

"Gina, Eric, Gina?" Christina timidly probed.

"Oh, now, watch yourself. I saw Gina and squashed everything between us. I told you I'm focused now and just ready for my career so everyone else has to get in where they fit."

"Eric, that is selfish. Just make sure you are being crystal clear with these women. You know we women sometimes have hidden agendas. And besides," Christina pressed her case, "whether you admit it or not, if you had all three women together, you are in a relationship, like it or not."

"Gotcha, gotcha, Chrissy. For real, I get it." Eric knew he couldn't debate with a woman. He'd take this "L" for the team. "Let's get together on your next trip this way."

"Eric, Eric." Christina wasn't ready to let him off the hook.

"What?" Eric really didn't want to know.

"Cut the substitutes."

"Christina, hear me clear. They are not substitutes. I've been celibate since college and the ladies are just my friends."

"Since college, or since Gina?" she challenged again. "Since you got your heart broke, you mean."

"Getting sick of being on trial here." Eric sighed and did his best to change the subject. "Hey, I heard from some guys from the old neighborhood Rico is out on parole. Be careful."

"Nice try, Eric. Yes, Rico is out on parole and I have a

restraining order. And I don't think he even knows I moved to New York City. Let's hope it stays that way. Thanks for asking. You know, Rico was my substitute for too long. If I had cut him out of my life sooner maybe..." Christina's voice drifted off.

Knowing it was better to concede than to keep the debate going, Eric said, "Okay, I'll really pray tonight and ask God if these women are my substitutes or truly my friends. And you just be careful out there. Deal?"

"Deal. Talk to you later, cousin. And, hey, I've missed this. I'm glad you and I are talking again." Christina yawned.

Eric glanced at the clock. 10pm. His cousin was three hours ahead, up way past her bedtime. "I agree. I've missed you, too—but not all the questions." He laughed. "Get some sleep. Night, night."

As promised, Eric took the opportunity to pray and ask God to reveal the people and things in his life that were substitutes. He even got down on both knees, something he rarely did because of the pain that lingered long after. He was about to go back to college. He knew this was not the time for distractions. By morning he hadn't heard any revelations from God so he thought he was in the clear.

Later that same day, his boss called and invited Eric to the company golf day. He said to bring a date if he wanted to. Eric immediately thought of Stacey. She knew how to play the corporate game. But then Barisia would get him a lot of attention. And Lynette was cool and laid back and would definitely be fun to hang with. He heard softly, "All are substitutes for me."

Shrugging off the words, Eric decided Stacey deserved the outing after all the nice events she'd taken him to, so he picked up the phone and invited her to attend. Stacey immediately put him on hold for at least five minutes. When she returned she said, "Mr. Washington, that will work with my schedule. I'll meet you there." In Stacey-speak that meant she had another meeting near the golf outing. It was all business with her. She was the classiest chick Eric had dated since his high school days with Jessica.

Jessica. She could have been his wife by now, but she had never spoken to him again after the Candace mess. He shook his head. That darn Chrissy, putting marriage into his mind.

At the golf outing Friday afternoon, Stacey and Eric were a hit. She had the best handicap of all the women attending. Both she and Eric got the "yes" votes from his senior management. When it was time for Stacey to leave, she grabbed Eric's hand, thanked him for the invite, and was on her way. Business as usual. But wait. She pulled back into her parking space, rolled down the window and said, "Eric, you want to go to the movies tomorrow?"

Eric loved her initiative. But he and Barisia had a movie date. "Can't tomorrow. Maybe Sunday."

Stacey looked down at her Blackberry. "Got a brunch and a dinner Sunday. I'll catch you later." The glimmer of a person was gone. It was back to business as she zoomed off.

Eric's boss walked up. "Your lady friend left too soon. We are going to the lounge for drinks and cigars. You coming?"

"She's not my lady, but I'll come in a second."

Eric suddenly felt a need to call Lynette. He hadn't talked to her all week and wanted to see how she was doing.

"Hello, beautiful." Eric always greeted Lynette that way because he felt she needed to know she was the real package inside and out.

She chimed in. "Hello, handsome!"

"Hey, haven't talked to you this week. Wanted to make sure all was good with you."

"Yes, E. Just focused, getting a lot of paperwork done." Lynette was a teacher and was always overwhelmed by paperwork and lesson plans.

"Okay. Got to run. Call you later," Eric excused himself.

"Eric, why did you even call?" Lynette asked.

"I told you, just to say 'hi' for a moment."

"K, whatever, man. Talk to you later."

What's her deal? Eric thought as he headed back to smoke a cigar with senior management.

After getting into bed that night he called Lynette back. They talked all through the night. He even forgot to pray or read his Bible before he went to sleep. He figured he'd catch up in the morning. Wrong! He woke around noon to a call from Barisia asking him to go shopping before dinner. Eric obliged. Not that he enjoyed going from store to store with a woman. But he did enjoy watching Barisia's coke-bottle figure get in and out of slinky dresses. Well, Eric was celibate, not dead. Barisia knew that, which is why after their weekly movie outing she was always willing to help him push the limits of how far he was willing to go.

Anyway, as Eric showered he tried to wash away the images of what Barisia would look like today. When he was grabbing his keys to lock up, he noticed his cell phone was flashing. Christina. He didn't even pick it up. He didn't want to share that he was about to go hang out with another substitute.

Okay, he could finally admit it. He could see clearly Barisia was a substitute. But not his girl Lynette, and definitely not all-business, no-play Stacey.

At the mall, Eric enjoyed playing bag-holder for Barisia, until they stumbled into a jewelry store. Apparently, it was Valentine's Day and Eric had completely forgotten. The jeweler immediately made assumptions and took them to the ring case. Barisia blushed while Eric felt his eyes threatening to pop completely out of their sockets.

"Look, we need to get going if we're going to get dinner before the movie time," he said, pulling Barisia by the hand. He excused them out of the store.

Barisia was noticeably confused and disappointed that he didn't want to daydream with her. Seated at dinner later, Eric decided to kill the night completely. He asked Barisia, "Do you want to get married?"

Thankfully, she recognized it was not a proposal, just a

general question. "Look, EWash, I thought it would be fun to try on rings and just, you know, explore the future. I wasn't trying to force a relationship or pressure you. I was just playing."

That was the problem. Everybody was just playing. Just fantasizing. Just trying to see what it would be like.

"I know that," Eric replied. "Because you can't force a relationship with me. I know exactly who I am and what I'm focused on right now, and a relationship is not part of it. I'm sorry. But just answer my question; do you want to get married?"

Barisia looking embarrassed. "Of course. Yes, Eric. I'm like every other woman you've met. I want to be married."

Eric looked at his plate, trying to figure out a nice way to shut down this substitute relationship. Right now. "Look Barisia, I like you. I enjoy your company. But I've misled you by hanging out with you on a regular basis and even compromised both of us on many occasions. But I have to be honest. Marriage is the farthest thing from my mind right now. And I don't want to hold you up if you desire to be married. You need to be spending time with a man who desires the same thing, and that man just isn't me. I'm sorry, but I'd be even more of a jerk if I wasted any more of your time."

Barisia looked up at the lights on the ceiling. She probably hoped if she looked up long enough no tears would roll down her face. She feigned a smile. "Thanks, E. You really know how to let a girl down gently. You could have at least told the truth that you were dating someone else. Admit it. What's her name, one of the women I always hearing you hanging out with? Lynette or Stacey? You've decided to make one of them your girlfriend?"

Eric couldn't believe her recordkeeping. But then again, he could. "You forgot to mention my admin at work and the girl on the first floor of my building."

Then in 5-4-3-2-1, the tears began to fall down Barisia's beautiful checks. Eric didn't know what to do so he scooted his chair closer to hers and grabbed her hands as if they were about to pray.

"I'm really sorry. Look into my eyes. Look at me," he demanded. "I am not dating anyone, because I'm really not ready. And I'm trying to make sure I'm not misleading you. Looks like I was or blocking you from receiving the special man God has just for you."

Barisia nodded and put her head on his shoulder. From ten feet away, Eric and Barisia's special moment looked like a proposal, not a fake date gone wrong. The violinists in the restaurants came to their table. After one song, Eric tipped them nicely and they left.

True to her curvy form, Barisia still wanted the movie after dinner. They picked a comedy. They needed some good laughs. Eric didn't feel too bad, thinking about how the real players rotate three or four women on the 90-day plan for sex or whatever and keep them all thinking they have a shot at the ring. He thought about his old roommate/landlord Troy. At least he wasn't like that.

As Eric drove Barisia home, he didn't dare share those thoughts with her. She'd had enough of a reality check for one night.

Settling into his apartment for the night Eric kept thinking, boy that was some drama. Then he started thinking about Stacey and how she asked him to a movie on Valentine's Day—today. Hmmm. Maybe she had the wrong idea, too, getting the big head. Since he was on a roll, Eric decided to call Lynette and Stacey and shut down whatever fantasies they might be having.

He called his girl Lynette but got her voicemail. He sent a text for her to call him ASAP. Then he called Stacey, who picked up the phone with, "Happy Valentine's Day!" Yep, thought Eric, she's feeling me, too!

"Look, Stacey, I appreciate all you've done to help me get into the political scene and networking, but uh, you need to find another James—" As in James Bond, their private joke. "—for your escort needs in the future."

"What? Where is this coming from?" Stacey wondered.

"Well, I just don't want there to be any mixed signals." Eric tried to gently suggest that she was into him.

"On your part or mine?" Stacey sounded bewildered.

"Uh, either." Eric decided to retreat. Either the girl was not going to own up to her feelings or maybe his ego had gotten too big.

"Mmm, okay, Mr. Washington. From now on I'll try to get you separate invites on your own and you can bring whomever you want to the events."

Oh no, here we go, Eric thought. Now she was going to think he had a girlfriend and didn't need her as an escort anymore. Why couldn't a heterosexual man just want to be alone? Why did it always have to be about another woman? He was a little upset, but decided after his earlier evening, no need to escalate the drama. "Stacey, that would be great! No need for me plus one. Table for one, thanks! I'm learning I'm good on my own at these things." He forced a laugh. "I can't use you as my social butterfly crutch forever."

A serious Stacey replied, "So true." He could tell she was writing this down in her day planner.

Then Eric heard Stacey's background. "Baby, are you coming back to bed?"

"Okay, Mr. Washington, thanks for the update." Eric could now see that she was in a hurry to end the conversation. "I've noted this and will operate accordingly."

"Al—alright, Stacey," Eric stuttered. "See you around."

Baby? Eric felt embarrassed. Stacey was truly okay with his status, single or otherwise. She just needed to update her list. Years later, Eric found out from mutual friends that Stacey was going to introduce him to a friend of hers. That's the only reason she'd invited him to the movie that day. In fact, Eric met her boyfriend at an event a few months later. He looked miserable. He told Eric he was just not into the monkey-suit business at all. He worked with his hands and liked to get dirty and hated going to Stacey's socialite events.

Woops. Okay, so Stacey wasn't into Eric after all. Just like she was for him, he was just her substitute.

The next morning, Eric got up early to run before getting ready for church. He figured since Lynette hadn't called back the night before, it must be a sign from above that she was in no way a substitute, but his true friend, his "homey macaroni."

As he was about to get ready for church, his phone light began to glow the words, "Homey Lynn."

"E, what's wrong?" Lynette sounded really concerned.

"Uh, besides you not calling me back after I texted you to call me ASAP? Nothing." Eric realized he sounded rather smug.

Lynette sighed. "Well, that's what you get for leaving cryptic text messages at almost midnight." She threw the blame right back in his lap.

"Oh yeah, well, it doesn't matter now." Eric wanted to just hang up so he could get back to what he was doing. Lynette would always be a close friend.

"No, tell me," Lynette pressed.

"Seriously, let it go. It was stupid." Eric really just wanted to put on his tie for church. Why did women always want to talk it out?

"Well, uh, I need to share something with you." She sounded nervous.

"Go for it. I'm really hoping it's worth me being late for service."

"You know it is! I know you remember me telling you about Kenneth." Lynette sounded excited.

"Yeah," Eric snickered. "The guy with bad breath that asked you out three times before you said yes when you put a mint in his mouth."

"Stop it! That was one time. And we've been going out off and on for almost six months. Well, last night he asked me to enter a six-month pre-engagement workshop called—"

"Table for 1," Eric interrupted. He recalled the first time he had heard those words before his mom and stepfather were married, and then again from Christina.

"How'd your lone-wolf-behind hear about that?" Lynette knew about his blog and poetry. Some women just didn't know when NOT to bring up a man's personal stuff.

"Go ahead with your story, Lynette."

"Well, I said yes. We are going to be taking the workshop on Saturdays and Sundays. But there was just one concern." She sounded sad. "Ken pointed out to me that he wanted resolve before we start classes."

"What?" He was being pulled into a longer conversation than he desired on a Sunday morning, but he really wanted to hear what she had to say.

"Kenneth has this ridiculous idea that I'm only with him because I can't be with you. He is really jealous of all the time we spend on the phone together. Can you believe it?" Her tone sounded frustrated.

Eric stopped pacing in front of his closet and sat on the bed. He looked at himself in the mirror. "I hate to admit it," he said, "but I can. Actually, that was the reason I left you the message last night. My cousin Christina, my pseudo-psychologist, pointed out you might be a substitute for me not having a real relationship—well, you and other people."

Lynette laughed, "Hold up. If anybody is a substitute we know it is Sexy Barisia."

"True, but substitutes come in many forms as I've been learning lately. As I think about what Kenneth said, that's real talk. If I ever get married I want my wife to be my best friend, and if you guys want a fair shot at building that you've got to make more time for you two. I mean, I guess." Eric was grudgingly letting go of his homey macaroni.

"Eric, let's just have you and Kenneth meet. Then I'm sure we'll all be one big happy family." Lynette was ready to package together a nice marriage of her, Eric, and Kenneth. But it wasn't going to work.

"Just make sure Ken is strapped with a role of Lifesaver mints," he quipped. "And how's Kenneth going to feel when he realizes I finish your sentences and know what you are thinking before he does?"

"Whatever. He already knows you aren't too bright. You are passing on a great woman right in front of you," she countered with a nervous joke of her own.

Eric almost forgot he was running late for church, but he knew this conversation marked a shift in their relationship. He hoped it didn't mean he was losing his homey. "Hey, Lynn, I got to head out. I'll see you at church, okay?"

Lynnette hesitated. "Actually, I'm starting to visit Ken's church now. I'll catch up to you later in the week."

Reluctantly, Eric had to admit he really must give his spiritual sister his blessing. "Lynn, let's make sure you get Ken and me to meet sooner rather than later. I mean, if he is really concerned, listen to him. So many of y'all women don't. If this is the only issue you have going into marriage, you guys are blessed. Cool?"

"Great! Thanks, Eric. I'm so glad you are truly an honorable brother."

Lynette sounded blissful as she thought all was right in the world. Eric and Ken went to dinner alone and then with Lynette. He and Ken were cool alone, but when all three were together there was no connection.

As Eric reflected over getting rid of his substitutes he thought it was funny; Stacey knew his mind, Barisia understood his body, but Lynette knew his heart and soul. That's why, though innocent for both of them, it was a fire waiting to be lit. He was glad they were able to diffuse it and keep some remnants of their friendship.

Over the next few months Eric reaped the benefits of cutting the substitutes from his life. Attending black-tie events without Stacey meant he actually talked to people he liked and not just because they were committed to Stacey's campaign fundraiser. Eric definitely missed Barisia's body and how it complemented him on many occasions. But he now had his mind free to focus on thoughts that were pure, lovely and of good report. And he had time available to pursue his Computer Science degree at night and on weekends.

On breaks from his studies his mind began to drift to what type of woman he would want to one day marry, especially as he observed his homey macaroni Lynette preparing for marriage. For the first time Eric began to feel the Genesis scripture, God says it is not good for man to be alone.

Genesis 2:18

The Lord God said, "It is not good for the man to be alone. I will make a helper suitable for him."

He tried to shrug off thoughts of his future wife. He still had almost two years to complete his second degree. Between work and doubling up on classes he had no time for a social life.

When he'd first moved near Silicon Valley he had purchased an old beat-up car for commuting back to San Diego at least once a month to play a game of basketball at the recreation center where he used to work and meet up with his old roommates. But as school heated up, this quickly came to a halt.

For years he had chased a basketball dream wrapped up in acquiring all those things the guys talked about. They were his substitutes, and in life we would always have some type of substitute for facing our real problems or avoiding a void.

In a strange way, even Eric's Lone Wolf blog was a substitute that kept him from sharing his heart and feelings with anyone. Every other week, he would find himself up at some insane hour, instead of calling Lynette, going to his blog to upload his heart to the world through his anonymous site.

Proverbs 4:23

Above all else, guard your heart, for everything you do flows from it.

He vowed from now on to guard his heart—and his blog— for that special woman who would be his wife; that is, if God decided he could handle such a beautiful rose called love between a husband and a wife. He knew only God's agape love could reconcile the thorns that come with love, as long as he kept God's love first and foremost. Inspired, he wrote in his blog:

The Defenseless Rose

A defenseless rose caught my eye
The rose was my heart causing me to draw nigh
A defenseless rose.
I saw I am, my flesh made me think I was doomed
For the rose, my heart, had never fully bloomed
The beauty of the rose was shadowed by thorns of
the past.
When I struggled to remove the thorns and see
The Lord revealed, the barrier was me
The barrier of substitutes were woven around my
heart.
They guarded me from the love God had right from
the start.
The substitutes I thought were my defense,
In reality were weeds killing my fence.
The weeds choked the thorn lined fence, which
brought pain.
God revealed the thorns were to bloom the rose and
not bring shame.
Then He showed me the rose's beauty was mine for
the taking,
But life choices made it difficult in the making.
Now I'm caught off in a war of emotions
Want to break free, but feeling lost in the oceans.
Cut the substitutes, I must confess and no longer
be afraid.
A defenseless rose, my heart is worth the price
Jesus paid.

Ding! *Eric awoke to hear "We are through the turbulent part. It is safe to unbuckle your seatbelts and move about the cabin.*

Part III: The Chair

"A Seat to Eat...A Position to Hear God"

Now we have arrived at the part in the book where I hope to make you hungry. However, the type of hunger pains is not what you might expect. I want you to have growling pains to know God and His word for yourself. I have yet to meet a man who didn't know how to get his grub on when it was time to eat food. But somehow when it is time to dine at the table for one with God at the head and to study to show yourself approved, men are not as eager. Why? I have found many men have been nurtured to believe that trusting the Bible over instinct or knowledge is a little weak. Others don't want to be confronted with the Word to face their foolish ways. So without knowing they can live eternally, they have chosen death even while yet appearing to be among the living. Of course, many a woman too has chosen this path. So invite you to the table where God is seated at the head. Take a seat. Sit still. Eat by studying the word of God.

II Timothy 2:15

[15] Do your best to present yourself to God as one approved, a worker who does not need to be ashamed and who correctly handles the word of truth.

But let's be careful to handle the word of truth with special care. For example, a sure way to turn some men completely off, ladies, is to show your scriptural literacy. Remember, you are the weaker vessel. Don't be afraid to show your frailty. This does not mean you should dumb down, but don't be so quick to show yourself studied up. For this reason, some men leave the fork on the table (since the woman knows it all) and the seats intended for the men are left empty.

This is no slight on men, just another observation from a woman by the grace of God in pursuit of a table for one. I believe this is the reason there are often more women than men in church, especially when it comes to active ministry. Just something to think about the next time you are eating the Word of God, or a good steak.

Back to business. Not that we are babies, but all of us at one time or another need someone else to "feed" us when we don't have the strength or know-how to get the Word for ourselves. I think it is harder to find men who acknowledge this need, not because they are rare, but because it is rare that men have safe places where they can be vulnerable without some type of "WEAK" label assigned to them.

In one of my interviews preparing for this book a man referred to desiring this safe place in his relationship with his girlfriend, but often she was so focused on downloading her day and her IPCs (issues, problems and concerns) he had no one to talk to and no place to share his own.

Often it is the older men, the men who have lived a very colorful life, who are picking up the forks and preparing themselves for their new season in life. But how awesome would it be if younger men began to rise up (even more than now) and feast on God's Word, causing a revival of young "honorable" men. Just picture that for a second or two, and then imagine the decline it would bring of youth crimes, murders, drug addiction and more.

We all need to eat for daily sustenance, but we especially need men to eat and prepare for God's blessings. Usually at this point of the book I encourage non-believers to continue reading to the very end to get what God has for them in the book. But instead, I will just say "eat." God desires for you to dine with Him.

Eating is more than studying God's Word and praying. It is also obedience to what you have read, heard and received from your "eating" time. Every man and woman should have an accountability partner to ensure their "eating" and obedience thereto will position them to receive all God has for them on earth and in heaven.

I pause now to encourage female readers to pray for men of God to encourage and hold accountable other men. Pray for healthy "accountability" not just between the older men and the younger men, but even among peer groups. One man wisely advised me not do business, marry or enter a close friendship with any man who doesn't have an earthly accountability partner or "check mate".

Fortunately for Eric, he found Coach Frank and Coach Riley. As he got older, there were certain things his mother was not going to be able to help him with, to "Man Up," so to speak. Right now Eric sees being a provider as the ultimate sign that he could be a good husband. Although that is a sign—and a good one, I might add—a more important sign is looking to dine at a table for two, as he is about to discover.

More than being a provider, he would need to:

- Effectually and fervently pray for his household.
- Act with a single-minded focus to please God first.
- To love his wife with his "whole" heart.

Was he really ready for all that? Let's find out.

Eric learns to eat
(Eric at 30 to 32)

Eric graduated with his second degree, but two years later he was still working in Sales. Tithing had really paid off, more than he ever imagined. But while he credited tithing for his improved financial stability, he still thought it might be that he was just good at Sales. So he decided to wait another year before moving over to the Software Engineering department.

A key to his success in Sales was his ability to effectively describe the company's software products to potential clients. He decided to use the company's reimbursements to work on his Master's degree that would definitely ensure he would not lose too much pay when he started over in the Software Engineering department.

Eric now had a little more time for a social life, but found himself really trying to get rest from his Sales trips and outings on the weekends. He still did the gym and pick-up games. And women? Eric met a nice woman every now and then, but they seemed too eager for his taste and he just couldn't get excited about them as the future Mrs. He was going to church; he just felt blah about it. He heard somewhere that if your church isn't changing you maybe you need to be changing churches. So one Sunday he visited a new church.

Funny, the pastor was doing a special sermon for Singles and admonishing them not to be "unequally yoked." He told the young ladies the first thing they needed to know is whether the men they date have a "Father" in heaven they are accountable to. He told the men to stop "running through the pews like there is toilet tissue attached to their feet." Eric got a good laugh, but he felt the pastor was more slanted toward helping the ladies than the men.

Then at of nowhere, at the end of the service, an "angel" appeared. She was escorting four pre-teen girls to their parents, delivering some type of note or permission slip to each. She was about 5'5" and definitely no stranger to the gym. Eric wanted to reach out and touch her arm as she passed him, but he didn't know what to say. And he definitely didn't want to be like the girls who used to pass him notes during offering at his old church. She walked by him a second time. This is it, Eric thought. He drew a breath to speak… But she didn't even look up once from her mission to get her kids safely to their parents.

Then the pastor called for no movement as he prayed. The angel obediently stopped and bowed her head. Hmm. Loves kids and submissive…

While the pastor prayed, Eric had to contain himself from preying on the angel. He bowed his head and said a private prayer of his own. He asked God that he might see her again one day. He'd never tell her about that prayer unless she turned out to be the one. The pastor, the congregation and Eric said "Amen."

She passed Eric a third time, this time holding out her envelope to an usher since she hadn't been able to turn in her offering while she was returning children to their parents. In his heart, Eric heard, that's the kind of focus I need you to have.

He didn't find a new church home that day. But he did find an angel, maybe the future Mrs. Washington.

Eric tried to put the woman out of his mind, but when he closed his eyes to sleep that night he saw her. Whoa! It had taken Gina only one night to get him, but this woman he had never even spoken to. He had never heard her speak and didn't even know her name. Yet she would haunt his dreams. Was she an angel or a distraction? He woke and prayed her out of his dreams.

The next morning, waiting for the train to work, he again tried to push her out of his mind in favor of plans for his week of work, trips and studies. Focus is what God wanted and focus is what he was going to ha... Suddenly, there she was. On the train. The angel—his angel?

She looked up at him and right back down as if she saw a ghost. That wasn't the usual reaction Eric got from a woman. He was indeed curious about this angel. But he could never get close enough to meet her.

This went on for weeks. Then one day on the crowded train Eric seized the moment. He slipped her a note like he was in elementary school. He even put a little check box next to his home phone and cell numbers, hoping to make the woman smile. But he watched his joke get stuffed unread into a jacket pocket.

She was definitely no angel after all. She didn't even look back. Maybe he hadn't been specific enough in his prayer.

When the train stopped, Eric collected his bag and tossed it quickly over his shoulder. Then he heard the angel speak.

"Eric Washington?"

Eric turned. He couldn't contain his joy. A big goofy grin burst out. Praise God his mom had worked her butt off to pay for braces.

The angel had a name. Brinly Daniels. And she was more an angel's agent than an actual angel. She unloaded questions that, thankfully, Eric felt equipped to answer.

"Do you know my Father?"

He immediately replied, pointing above without missing a beat, because it had been a part of the sermon for singles he had heard from her pastor when he visited her church. Thankfully, Brinly had entered his line of sight after he'd heard the part of the message about how singles needed to be equally yoked and how if a man doesn't know your heavenly father he doesn't need to know you. Eric smirked to himself. If Miss Brinly only knew he didn't just know the Father, he'd asked His permission before he ever spoke to her. Once again, he opted to keep that detail to himself.

Three months went by. Eric couldn't believe it—Brinly was not perfect, but somehow he still saw her as an angel, a sweet angel whose heart he didn't want to break. He didn't want to lose her.

Eric hadn't really thought too much about marriage or "the one" until his cousin Christina had started challenging his "substitutes." Then his homey macaroni Lynette pulled back to focus on her courtship, now engaged to Kenny. A part of him was falling for Brinly just out of finally knowing what it meant to be alone. After all, the Bible said it is not good for man to be alone. Now Brinly had entered the scene as the queen for which he had no solid biblical idea what it meant to be her king and head.

During his talks with Brinly in those few short months she shared more nuggets from her pastor's sermon series "Naked & Unashamed" for singles and married couples to experience the Garden of Eden before the fall. Eric took mental notes for his blog on the characteristics of a man ready to be married:

1. Fears God (Obedience).
2. Is not afraid of marriage.
3. Can admit his faults, mistakes and when he's hurt you.
4. Controls his passions.
5. Honors his parents.
6. Is growing in leadership and knows how to serve.

Eric wanted that, maybe even with Brinly. But he knew it required him not just knowing how to get and keep a job, but having a vision for the provision. And right now that just wasn't where he was. What he had shared with Christina about not being ready was true, but it was not for the reasons he initially thought. It was not about completing his degrees, increasing his income, or achieving things he wanted to accomplish. He needed to be still before God and learn more about who he was as a future husband and father. First he had to be the son God was calling him to be.

As he thought more about truly being a son in God's eyes, Eric began to see the challenge was not that he didn't know how to study God's Word and learn what it meant to be a head. The problem was growing up. He was raised around just women. His biological father—just a sperm donor—had left before Eric turned one year old. And his grandfather had died when he was six. Eric never had a man as an example— good or bad—of how to be a father, husband or even a true son.

He knew Brinly tried to picture what had been like for him to have grown up without a relationship with a biological father. But she really couldn't understand what he was going through. He had been with her on several occasions when her own father called her. She curled up on the couch as if she were still seven years old. Eric knew his dad lived in California, but wasn't sure he would recognize him if they passed on the street.

These new revelations overwhelmed Eric and he didn't even know who to go to. His stepfather? His old coach? His single roommates in San Diego? Definitely his mom and cousin Christina were out of the question. They hadn't learned what his spiritual gifts were, let alone all the many gifts there were in the body of Christ.

There had been enough false starts in Eric's career. He didn't want any false starts when it came to getting into a serious relationship.

He visited Brinly's church a few more times and agreed with the pastor's teaching. The very clear pathway was friendship, courtship, and then marriage. After three or four months, Brinly would be looking for Eric to set the tone and state his intentions. She was a queen. And although he liked her—maybe even loved her—he knew he was not ready to be her king. Besides, he'd even been preparing to do missions during his vacations how would she'd react to that, he wasn't ready to share that part of himself yet.

Furthermore, he still had one class to finish the certification he needed for his IT position and he wanted to go on and complete his Master's degree. He was tired of being a benchwarmer at church. He'd been trying to find the right job and make the right pay for so many years he'd bypassed opportunities to be still with God and know what was his office in Christ should be that no job or man could replace.

He knew from that sermon at Brinly's church about headship that he should have a vision before he got married. Other than one day being an officer of the company, Eric had no clue on a vision for himself, let alone for a wife or family.

Facing this realization, Eric turned on the lamp beside his bed and took out his IPad. He opened his Lone Wolf blog and wrote:

Hearing God to Rule While Seated

I struggle to hear God's voice and begin to pray.
No strange voices while I attempt to hear deep beyond the fray.
Hearing His voice, I must obey and search within.
It's this voice filled with love, keeping me from sin.
Telling me I'm a conqueror go forth and begin.

Beginning again, deeper relationship with Him, lose myself, none of me
I realize the principle of ONE has manifested as ME becomes WE!
I want, what God wants for me, more than what I want for myself.
By His spirit the soil of my heart is damp and moist to reap His wealth.

Hearing and obeying His voice is the secret to ruling while seated
Along with cutting off interferences that would leave me depleted
I sit before the Lord and open His sword
Ruling becomes a position and His will to restore

He was feeling the Lord's call to missions. Eric didn't know how to articulate to Brinly his feelings, especially his areas of deficiency. He just didn't know enough about his future. So he gradually let their budding relationship fade to black. And that's when Eric went on his first mission trip a few years earlier.

"Thank you for flying with us. Welcome home."

Eric jerked out of his sleep. Drawn out of his past, he realized his present—getting kicked off the mission field. It wasn't that bad, was it? If reconnecting with Brinly wasn't blessing enough, he now knew for sure all things work together for the good of them that love God, who are called according to his purpose. Maybe God just had him revisit the beginning of his walk to appreciate where God had him now.

Part IV: The Table

"Write the Vision"

King David, after many times of trying to set his own vision or run with his own plan that he thought matched the vision God had given him, surrendered to God's lead. In the third verse of the 16ᵗʰ Psalm he wrote,

> *"Commit thy works to the Lord and He shall make thy plans established."*

All of us have dreams and visions. Many of them were instilled in us by God. But without a plan—or should I say plans—to bring the vision to life, they are often blown away by the winds of life or destroyed during a stormy season. The Bible says in the first part of **Proverbs 29:18,**

> *"Where there is no vision, the people perish."*

Before two can become one it is important to understand who you are and the vision God has designed for your life. It helps shapes the new vision you and your mate will have together.

As I interviewed men I found that when it comes to setting a vision there are mainly three categories of men: 1) the man with a plan, 2) the limited plan man and 3) the man without a plan. It is amazing how the enemy uses this heavy weight of "setting the vision" to scare men, or should I say to confuse them to the point where no decision about marriage is made.

Please note, I am not using these titles to label or condemn. And I know there is a woman's side to each of these categories. Now back to what I've learned about men setting the vision at the table for one to a table for two.

First, the man with a plan. This man is resolved to fulfill his personal vision and plan before he even gets married. He makes declarations such as, "I will not get married until I have one million dollars in the bank." He can't comprehend that the vision is for an appointed time, one part for singleness and one part for married life, or that the "favor" he would gain from choosing the right wife would be more valuable than a million dollars in the bank.

Next there's the limited plan man. While he's grasped the concept of the vision and making a plan he won't implement it for fear of failure. He is frozen by insecurities, and let's just say "he doesn't want to." That is until the right woman comes along. Then and only then will he sit up straight at the table and lay out the vision. He will do it so well his ex-girlfriends are like, "Really? Him?"

Finally, there's the man with no plan. I believe this is the man God wants to use the most. This man has no clear vision, he just knows marriage is a part of it and can't understand why he hasn't met "the one." Maybe that is a blessing. Maybe God wants him to be able to "set the table/vision" for his wife-to-be.

Side note: That's why many women are attracted to men in leadership positions or with special gifts and talents. It's never the looks. They just look at the "glitter" and don't want the flames that come with getting that gold to shine.

As I interviewed men for this book, I found one common thread for the men that were indeed preparing to be married. They had taken time to get before God on His vision for their lives, both as a single men and married men.

I also found one common thread for men—and even women—who found themselves single again. They had no clear vision on who God had called them to be as singles and who God had called them to be as married.

While this is imperative for both men and women, it is a critical part of a man's journey to setting his table for one, for he is called to be the head of the marriage covenant, and as the head he has the awesome mantle, kingdom assignment, to set the vision. Two biblical truths reflecting the importance of vision:

> **Proverbs 29:18** *"Where there is no vision the people perish.";* and ***Habakkuk 2:2*** *"Write the vision…"*

Unfortunately, that's what's happening in the world today. The vision is not written down and it is the last thing people discuss before getting married. For women, it is usually limited to living out a childhood fantasy, and for men, to a television show they saw a time or two. The vision is not committed to the Lord and is limited to deciding where they should live and who's paying which bill. This ultimately leads to divorce or the helpless caption, "It's complicated."

Now, with God all things are possible and He is gracious. I know many marriages that have benefited from His grace and mercy while neither spouse had taken time to invest in setting their own table for one. God joined them together and is perfecting their life together. But each person knows what God has shown them and revealed to them and they will be held accountable to that regardless of what happened with the "Jones's marriage."

Often I've thought, well Lord, they got to do it and they were blessed. Meditate on this verse from Luke 12:48: "From everyone who has been given much, much will be demanded; and from the one who has been entrusted with much, much more will be asked." You will be judged according to what you "know."

To my female readers, I admonish you not to confuse the "men-u-see" for "men-i-stry." Men are attracted to you for the God in you, not for you at all.

Now back to the three types of men. Which do you think Eric

is? Let's find out and see what attracted Brinly to this man.

Eric writes the vision

By the time Eric had collected his bags at the airport the abrupt end of his mission trip had taken a back seat to his excitement about the potential for him and Brinly. In the cab ride home he thought about how Brinly wouldn't be home for four months, enough time for him to pick out, save for and purchase an engagement ring.

A ring? Yes, Eric was ready, and he didn't want to waste any more time. If anything, his dreams on the flight home made him unwilling to waste one more day, especially concerning Ms. Brinly Marie Daniels.

Eric put the key in his apartment door, ready to pass out on his comfy leather couch. He dropped his bags, turned on the big flat-screen television and threw himself on the couch. Immediately, he drifted off to sleep.

He awoke a few hours later to the sight of a half-naked woman crossing the room. Barisia! Oh, no! In his rush to return home he had completely forgotten about Barisia. His "old friend," was subletting his apartment while he was in Chile. He expected she would be married by the time he returned. He covered his eyes.

"I don't remember leaving the TV on," Barisia said as she entered the room. She shut the television off.

His eyes still covered, Eric said, "Barisia, don't freak out."

Barisia hadn't noticed Eric on the couch or his luggage near the door. She started screaming!

"Don't scream," Eric said calmly. "I barely saw anything. I covered my eyes."

"Eric!" Barisia yelled. "What are you doing here?" She ran toward the guest room and returned wearing a bathrobe."

Oh boy, Eric thought. This would be hard to explain to Brinly. He would just have to make sure Barisia left as they originally agreed, which was at least two months before Brinly returned home.

The next morning Barisia surprised Eric by cooking breakfast. She poured him coffee and put all his mail in front his plate, noting the certified mail notice on top of the stack.

Eric grabbed it first, realizing it was an envelope from the company he had worked for since moving to Silicon Valley. They had been understanding of Eric's needs to give back, allowing him to take a four-to-six month leave of absence twice in the past four years. He assumed it must be his leave paperwork and what he needed to do to be reinstated once he returned. He tucked the slip into his wallet. He could take care of that on Monday.

In the meantime, he needed to figure out his plan to pursue and finally marry Brinly. His living arrangement with Barisia was not the best idea.

While Eric was lost in thought, Barisia was chatting away.

"Eric, Eric are you listening to me? Babe don't do that. You know I missed you."

She reached for his hand. Though she was engaged, Barisia had always been a touchy-feely girl. Immediately, Eric jerked his hand away. He wanted to honor their agreement, but he would have to go ahead and tell her about Brinly and how their roomie situation was not ideal.

By the time Monday arrived, Eric was confident he knew how to be a Christian single man, whole and holy, even with a female roommate. Did he pray about that? Of course not. Besides, Eric barely remembered the last time he'd had sex. Well, it was with Barisia, but that had been at least four years ago.

He called his buddies to try to find another place for Barisia, but the only one with a room was his friend Troy, the playa for life, that lived five hours away. He would just have to live with the roomie situation.

Eric decided to go back to work as soon as possible, especially so he could get Brinly the ring she deserved. Instead of calling his boss or team and sharing his early return, he decided to surprise his boss. He'd bring lunch for the team and they'd talk about his transition plan to come back full-time within the next week or so.

Eric put on his Jos. A. Banks suit with a Brooks Brothers pin-stripe shirt, a tie and for a touch of bling, his gold cufflinks with the EW monogram. He left the apartment early so he'd have time to stop at the post office and get his leave-of-absence package on his way to the office. He called his admin, Kelly, to ask her to place an order for his team with a local deli around 11 o'clock. He'd pick it up as he drove in to surprise his boss and co-workers.

"Eric, what are you doing coming in?" Kelly asked. She sounded almost irate.

"Calm down," Eric said. "I'll explain when I get there. But for now, make sure the team is in the conference room and I'll surprise them with lunch."

Kelly sounded shocked. "You really want to do that?"

Eric assured Kelly everything would be okay once he explained and hung up the phone. He pulled out his ear piece with his left hand and pushed the car ignition with his right. But as he heard the hum of the engine of his two-year-old VW, he felt strange, and it wasn't the engine. Eric's tie suddenly felt too tight. His shirt was causing him to sweat, and it was cool outside.

To settle himself, Eric pushed the ignition button off and just sat looking at himself in the rearview mirror. He had to shake off this strange feeling. He hadn't taken time for his dedicated confession time that morning where he would recite positive affirmations from the Bible concerning his life. Over the years with Coach Frank, Eric had learned the power of confessing the truth no matter how things might feel or look at the time.

Thinking his feeling had to do with Senor Perez and Chile, Eric said a quick prayer asking God to remove any residue of bitterness about the way his good work was thrown out in Chile, how quickly the schoolmaster had forgotten the awesome lab he had created. Okay, the awesome lab God had used him to create. But then Eric remembered Brinly. It would all be worth it if that is what it took to find his wife and claim her for his own.

Eric smiled at himself in the mirror as if he were looking at Brinly. He turned on his favorite CD and restarted the car.

After stopping at the post office to pick up his certified mail, Eric headed to Silicon Valley. He let the sunroof back to feel the breeze on his head. Instead of the CD, he decided to turn on the satellite radio sports station to hear about the basketball playoffs. He thought back to the time when basketball had been his whole life and thanked God for leading him to his true passion, technology.

When Eric arrived at the deli, they told him the order placed by Kelly was not ready, so he pre-paid and told them to bring the big order to his car when it was finished. He'd chill out in the car and listen to the sports updates.

He noticed the thick package from his company in the passenger sit. It seemed thicker than his he expected. Intuitively, he reached to open it to get a head start on the human resources runaround he would have to work through when he got to the office. He loved his company, but when it came to protocol and order they were so paperwork driven. As the saying goes, "If it isn't written down, it didn't happen."

Just then there was a tap at his window. The order was ready. Eric sat the bag on the floor of the passenger side and headed to the office. Odd, his admin Kelly was waiting outside and escorted him into the office past security, swiping for him since his hands were full. Eric thought that was really sweet. She must have missed him.

She was walking so fast though, like she didn't want anyone to see Eric. She ushered him into the conference room. "Eric, why on earth are you here?"

Eric thought about explaining the missionary fiasco, but he left it at, "I missed you guys so I decided to come back early."

Kelly said, "I hope you don't think this is going to change anything."

"What would I want to change?"

"Eric, I know you've been home a few days now. You must have received your lay-off package."

Eric felt like he was in a tunnel. The word "lay-off" seemed to echo over and over in his head. He felt as if someone had just sucker-punched him in the stomach.

"Oh, no." Kelly put her hand to her forehead. "You didn't know. Steve said he called you and left a voicemail for you to talk to him before you checked your mail."

Eric was still stuck on the words "lay-off." He looked down at his phone and realized he'd only used it to call Kelly. He'd been so completely immersed he hadn't even bothered to check his full voicemail because he figured all those messages would have waited three months so surely they could wait three days.

Steve, Eric's boss, arrived at that moment. "Son, we need to talk. Thanks for the lunch, but not sure you really want to be with the team today."

Did he really just say son? The word he hated for any older man to call him? Eric looked his boss in the eyes. "Steve, I'm not your son. You must have known this was coming. You knew before I left. How could you let me leave without telling me?"

Steve just shook his head. "I asked you if you were sure this was the right timing, that you could be promoted by the end of the year if you stayed."

Eric tried to keep his voice at a normal octave, but it rose as he said, "Yes, I recall, 'promotion this year or next' being the only thing at stake. I don't recall, 'stay and get promoted or leave and get fired.'"

Steve held up his hands for Eric to calm down. "Look, Eric.

The team is about to come in for lunch. Kelly was nice enough not to tell anyone you were coming. You can either be escorted out by security or we can make this a nice mini-going-away party for you. It's up to you. What role do you want to play?"

The words, "role you want to play," rung in Eric's ears. Steve was trying to play it cool. This was the most down-to-earth and real he had ever heard the man speak—even to his children. But his choice of words reminded Eric of the beginning of his training days with Coach Frank.

Eric could not change Chile, or the layoff, but he could control his response. In a flash, Eric recalled how when he played his role as the team leader the team won a championship. This wasn't a game, but he knew he needed to play his role and leave on the best terms possible.

"I'm sorry Steve," he muttered. "I'm out of line. This just caught me off guard. I didn't get your voicemail and I hadn't opened the certified package. I just picked it up." Eric was remorseful. This was not the role he wanted to play.

Steve smiled nervously. He looked like he was still ready to call security. Then he slapped Eric on the back. "Alright. Let's have that going-away party."

The party lasted all of twenty minutes. The team wished Eric well and went back to their respective projects. Wow, the love! Eric thought. Kelly was nice enough to arrange a visitor's badge for Eric to clean out his cubicle. He could stay in the main conference room the rest of the day. He shredded hard copy files, deleted files on his company computer and backed-up others on flash drives. He gave away operational manuals and other training documents that were proprietary.

Thinking this was not the day he had planned at all, he decided to go through his official package. Thank goodness he did. He read through the first paragraph. It stated he was entitled to only three month's severance. But that wasn't what hurt the most. It was the closing paragraph. It said he had only until today's date to respond if he wanted to take his vested money or it would be rolled over.

Eric reached for the phone to call human resources. The voicemail recording said they closed at 4pm. Eric's eyes burned with tears, but he wouldn't dare let them come down. Besides, he hadn't cried since high school when he'd found out his mother was marrying his stepfather. But that was a long time ago.

For the next hour, Eric sat in the conference room calling every manager he'd ever had lunch with, trying to get someone to be an advocate for him to help him get his money out of the company's fund. He knew with the current state of the job market he was looking at being out of work at least six months. He would need that money.

At that moment, his cell phone started ringing. Without checking to see who it was, he pushed his earpiece on.

"Hey, babe." It was Barisia. "I'm cooking. Just wanted to know if you are putting in a late one tonight at work."

Her "babe" made him smile just a little. "I'll be home by seven, Barisia." And just like that Eric made a plan for dinner with his fake wife. In the numbness of the crisis, thoughts of Brinly were forgotten.

Barisia was a great cook. She was a teacher and had gotten home from work early enough to grade papers and make a full spread for dinner. Eric needed that—or so he thought. He told her briefly about being laid-off. She didn't push the subject. She just reminded him that her brother was a recruiter if he needed help with his job search.

After dinner, they retired to their separate rooms. That's what Eric loved about Barisia. He didn't have to talk much or give details. Brinly would have pushed him to explain. But then again, Brinly really cared. She also would have made it a matter of prayer. He smiled thinking about her.

He charged up his personal laptop which hadn't been taken out of his luggage from Chile. Sure enough, Brinly was online. They got on Skype and talked until Eric drifted off to sleep and Brinly got ready to teach the kids in her classroom.

Brinly tried to probe Eric about whether he was going to end his leave-of-absence and return to work or enjoy some time off. Eric knew he could never turn back if he started lying to her, but he didn't want to tell her what was going on. Besides, she was thousands of miles away. By the time she returned Barisia would definitely be gone and hopefully he'd be close to landing a job or already have one. But Brinly got into her get-it-done mode.

"Is there anything else going on?" she asked. "You sound different, even a little bit irritated."

Eric sighed. Brinly could always read him. "Just pray, Ms. Brinly. Pray, okay? We'll talk when you get home."

Brinly seemed reassured, at least for the moment. Peace. Be still.

Eric and Brinly began to email and instant message like crazy, both high with the thought that in a few short months they could be together with no missionary agreements in the way. They would be officially courting when she returned home. But facing unemployment, Eric could not see how he could even pretend he was ready to be somebody's head of the table so to speak. So he slowed down on returning her emails and his instant email dates came to a screeching halt.

Brinly wondered what was going on with Eric. It seemed their relationship was finally on track. But when Eric seemed to be slow about communicating, she tuned in more to her missionary captain, Juan. Juan was so polite, so chivalrous. And although he didn't violate the missionary agreement on dating he always made sure Brinly was his right-hand for special assignments into the city or at other churches. He wouldn't try anything, but he gave her a knowing smile that made her forget all about Eric's slowdown. Besides, she thought, God was still first for her. Everything else would be as it was supposed to be.

Meanwhile, Eric became frustrated with his job search. It frustrated him that Brinly didn't keep emailing him to see what had happened to their usual two-hour Friday night instant message dates. Eric went to his anonymous Lone Wolf blog he had been keeping since college to write about the issues of his heart. But that wasn't enough to ease his feelings. So he got on his knees for the first time in a while and asked God to show him what to do now.

God simply reminded him the roadmap of his life before

Brinly. It was the only way he would know how to move forward with her, regardless of life's circumstances. Eric realized he'd spent most of his life compartmentalizing his past hurts instead of reflecting and learning from them. God wanted him to go back and remember what made him a solid, dependable, single and whole man ready for a table for two.

With his temporary roomie Barisia at work, Eric sat alone in his apartment. He was doing what he had learned to do best over the past three months—looking for jobs online and networking with recruiters by phone. It was amazing how quickly his days passed, and he hadn't been to the gym or enjoyed a day of rest in a long time. So there he sat, clicking around on Indeed.com for the fourth time in the day.

He had recognized a science to the postings—early in the morning, noontime, mid-afternoon and late evening. Eric was determined to have a job by the time Brinly returned from her mission trip so he could officially propose. They had Skyped the night before, and she said she would be home in the next week, but wouldn't give him an exact day. So as he attached his resume to a job posting for a position he knew he didn't like and he was overqualified for, he heard a gentle whisper.

"The answer is not on Indeed.com. It is in me."

Eric froze. God was telling him to pray over the posting before he uploaded his resume and submitted the application. He prayed and then hit the button to submit. Suddenly, his notepad crashed. He waited a few seconds and tried again. And again. And again. Then he heard the whisper again.

"The answer is not on Indeed, but in me."

Realizing this was not about "indeed.com" but that God indeed wanted to talk to him, Eric went to his room and got down on his knees. He began to worship the Lord until he could feel his Spirit increase and his worries decrease. He prayed and even cried out before the Lord, repenting, realizing He had committed three months to looking for work without once asking God if this was part of the vision for his life in this season.

He knew Brinly was his wife and he had to be a provider for her. So wasn't his job as a husband to fix the provision problem?

That's when God showed him, "Your job is not be the provider of money alone, but of the vision for your family and ministry."

God showed Eric the vision to be a good caretaker like his stepfather was for his mother. God showed him his stepfather did not just provide financially for his mom and brother, he was the chief prayer warrior. He sets up plans way in advance to prepare for changes in their lives.

Eric remembered when his stepfather had told him he wouldn't have to pay for his college education. It wasn't that he materially paid for it, but he was in the position that allowed Eric to be blessed with a free education. Eric realized he was trying to just apply for any job to fix a money problem, but he needed to be led by God to the kingdom position God wanted him to be in for his wife and family.

Not usually much for fasting, Eric felt led to do so. Before Brinly came home he must ask her not only to be his wife but to join him in this new vision. There it was. All this time he hadn't told Brinly about losing his job because he didn't want her to worry, and in his pride he wanted to show her he was a man with a plan and had already figured things out.

He wanted to be perfect for her. After all their times of back and forth this needed to be a smooth transition. Thankfully, God stepped in to show Eric the transition can't occur without the Chief Change Agent.

Eric remembered Brinly sharing with him years ago about "Choosing the Right Fast" (Isaiah 53). So he asked the Lord how he should fast and he heard he should choose a three-day fast with no food or water. And he had to be alone. No phone, and to his pain, no notepad either.

He quickly left Brinly a message on Skype before he shut it down then locked it in his desk drawer.

By the time Barisia returned home from work, he had booked a room near the airport and left a note on the counter that he would be gone for a few days. He knew Barisia would be confused, but she had enough worries of her own since her fiancé had been deported to Mexico and she hadn't heard from him. Hopefully, she wouldn't be too concerned about Eric's absence. She'd probably just go to bed early.

Brinly's Welcome Home

Brinly was hyped to be back to San Francisco. She'd missed her friends, her ministry and her architectural firm. Well, work, not so much. She was actually most excited about seeing Eric and continuing the conversations they've been limited to twice a week on Skype.

She wanted to surprise Eric. Saturday mornings he had his basketball games, so she asked Serena to pick her up from the airport. She'd go home, change and surprise Eric by the time he was back in the early afternoon.

When Serena picked her up, Brinly screamed to see how much "JJ," Serena's son, had grown. The two-year-old stood well above her knee. In spite of Serena's petiteness, his dad, Justin, was 6'6" after all.

Serena and Brinly chatted about the mission for a few minutes then Brinly told her she'd reconnected with Eric over there. Serena didn't seem surprised. "I wasn't sure you two would meet up, but I prayed," she said.

"Huh?" Brinly was confused.

Serena shared more about the matrix she was involved in. A few years ago, when Brinly had left Eric outside the restaurant in the rain as her cab drove away, Justin had begun a conversation with Eric and they'd become friends. Justin was probably at basketball with him right now.

What? This was all news to Brinly.

"But the missionary meet-up, that was all God," Serena added. "I promise. I had no idea Eric was going there or that he had been involved with that organization for a few years."

Neither did she, Brinly thought. In fact, there were many things she still didn't know about Eric.

"Brinly, before you get all super-spy," Serena cautioned, "remember men don't just open up in one day. This is a marathon, not a sprint you are in with Eric. Just keep the pace."

Brinly nodded, shaking off her feelings of being out of the loop and somewhat sideswiped. She got home and saw her short-term tenant had already vacated and actually left it immaculate, even better than when she left. She dropped her bags, ready for a shower after her long flight. She couldn't wait to see Eric.

Next she went to the fridge. How nice of the young lady to leave a case of water. She grabbed one and noticed her phone message light blinking. She saw one call was from her parents and the other from her BFF Jackie.

She went out to grab a cab since she'd given up the lease on her car. Heading to Eric's, she looked on her cell phone and thought about Skyping him to pretend she was still in Chile and be at his door at the same time, but thought that would ruin the surprise.

The cab driver stopped and asked if he should come back. Knowing Eric had a car and assuming he would be willing to drop her back home, Brinly let him go. She walked up the steps, gently smoothing her skirt to make sure she was not one bit wrinkled. She entered the building with another person going in and thought how lucky to keep the surprise going.

She knocked

"Just a minute!" A woman's voice.

She must have the wrong address. Brinly looked at the one piece of snail mail she'd convinced Eric to write her and saw it was from this address. Unit number 1007.

"Eric, is that you? Did you lose your key when you ran..."

The voice drifted off when she saw Brinly's owl-wide eyes and heard her challenging, "Who are you?"

Barisia's long black hair spilled out of the towel wrapped around her head. She appeared to be completely naked under her tightly-sashed bathrobe.

Barisia looked Brinly over as if she were a clerk at Wal-Mart, "Did you just knock on my door?"

"Uh, I'm sorry, I, uh, was looking for my, my..." She suddenly realized Eric hadn't officially said they were anything yet. "...my uh, my friend." Her south-Chicago accent was showing more than she intended. "My friend wrote me a letter with this return address. I—I was surprising him. My name is…"

At that moment, Brinly looked down and saw Barisia's engagement ring catching the light in the hallway. How stupid could she be? Eric's track record of pulling disappearing acts came to mind. She was too old for this and wasn't about to explain to his girlfriend—fiancé—wife, who knew?

Brinly turned on her heel and began to run to the elevator.

Then the woman started to call her. "Brinlia?"

What in the world? Eric had the nerve to give the woman some jacked-up version of her name? The elevator doors opened and she heard the apartment door slam behind her.

Outside Brinly remembered she had chosen to let her cab go. She would need to walk at least three blocks to get to a busy area where she could catch another, and she had worn her "get-it-girl" pumps. She was reliving a bad scene from her twenties.

As she began to walk she saw the woman coming out of Eric's building. She increased her pace. CRACK! Her heel broke. Could this get any worse?

"Brinlia, si?" the woman called.

"It's Brin-lee," Brinly articulated, fighting an embarrassing tear.

The woman kept pursuing her. "I know this looks crazy to you, but I've been friends with Eric for years. My name is Barisia. I was just subletting while Eric was in Chile. Then he lost his job and I had already pre-paid so he didn't make me move out."

As the woman rattled off all these updates on Eric, Brinly felt a flood of emotions—sadness, anger, perplexity. Who was Eric? More importantly, where was Eric?

Barisia continued her commentary about Eric's cryptic note explaining his needing to be alone with God for a three-day fast. Brinly was so confused.

When Brinly finally stopped trying to hobble away, Barisia offered to drive her back to her house. Reluctantly, Brinly accepted. If anything, maybe she might learn a little more about the man she thought was "the one." She was still a little foggy, but how could Eric have hidden such major life changes and decisions from her? She decided right then and there Eric was a liar, and she hadn't waited this long to marry a liar.

Barisia pleaded with Brinly. "I know Eric was going to tell you everything face to face. And I know it seems weird, but he did all of this for you." She looked down at her engagement ring as if she knew what that felt like.

Brinly, usually compassionate, usually willing to hear what's going on with someone else, nodded and said, "Best to you on your engagement."

"Just be open to Eric," Barisia pleaded as Brinly got out of the car. "He will open up in his own time."

Unaware that Barisia's fiancé had been deported and she had no clue when they would be married, Brinly was fuming. But even more than her anger, she was overcome with sadness. Heating a frozen dinner in the microwave, she sat down to once again ask God to give her joy, purpose and victory at a table for one.

While Brinly is confused and cloudy, Eric catches a New Vision

After day one of his three-day fast at his mini-retreat, Eric was on such a spiritual high. He kept his phone turned off and didn't check emails to see if recruiters had responded to his job inquiries. He was consumed with studying the Word and hearing what God was trying to speak to him. He grabbed the white board from the trunk of his car that he'd hurriedly packed up from his job.

He began to copy notes from an old journal and write them in order on the board, tracking spiritual and material milestones in his life. He realized the importance of the words he heard on the plane: "Go back to the beginning." He thought about what that meant on so many levels.

By the end of day two he knew he didn't want to work for another company full-time. He wanted his own business, but for what?

Eric began to make lists of all the ways he could consult or contract. Then God showed him Brinly and he was reminded of all her gifts and talents and how they could help one another. Eric was so relieved. At first he'd thought God was showing him all he needed to do before he could get married. Now he began to see the shape and form of marriage ministry.

He was excited and prayed over all the ideas. They included starting a virtual learning center for at-risk youth and high school dropouts and even an afterschool program for youth. He began to connect all the work he had done overseas and with youth in San Diego to his IT career. He knew Brinly loved working with youth and knew it was her secret passion to work with them full-time. Even her architecture skills would come in handy in designing a vocational school or teaching the next generation.

Then he saw her as a mom and really became overwhelmed with how this vision would lend itself to allowing more work/life balance in raising a family. Eric smiled, proud of himself, but realizing he could not take any glory, for this was truly God's vision and plan for him and his future.

Eric checked out of his hotel early Sunday and spent the day on the Wharf, opting to go to evening service. He closed his three-day fast reading **Jeremiah 29:11**

> : *"...a future, a hope and an expected end..."* *with the seals clapping and making noise in the background.*

Knowing Barisia had a tendency to get too relaxed when he wasn't around, Eric decided to call her cell to tell her he would be home in a few minutes. When he turned on his phone an explosion as texts came flying in from the north, south, east and west—most of them from Barisia. There were two from Brinly and even one from Justin, Brinly's old friend and his new buddy for pick-up basketball.

Strange, Eric thought. Justin usually called once a month or so when he could get, as he called it, "a pass" from his wife. Eric immediately opened Brinly's message first.

"I have a surprise being shipped to your door at noon today."

He didn't have time to wonder about that because the next text said, "Surprise was on me! May God bless you."

Eric knew "May God bless you," was Brinly's abbreviated version of, "May the Lord watch between me and thee while we are absent one from another."

Nothing like Brinly scorned. Eric was like, what?

Then he saw urgent messages from Barisia. "Call me ASP!" She had apparently been texting so fast she left out the second A.

Eric began to put the picture together and called Brinly several times on her cell, but never got through. He couldn't seem to dial back the number she dialed from. It was marked private. Eric thought, she must be really mad. He kept receiving the message, "This phone does not accept incoming calls."

He drove home, continually hitting redial on his steering wheel Bluetooth for Brinly's cell to no avail. Then he remembered the vision and realized this was just an attack against the vision that had been released. He decided to stop calling and just wait for God to work on Brinly. That was his only help.

Once in his apartment, he dropped his backpack and turned

on the light. He found Barisia crying. Oh God, more female drama. Not now, not now, he thought. But he asked, "Hey, homie, what's going on?"

"It's Josue," she answered. "He's…he's not getting cleared to return to the U.S. I will have to find a job in Mexico."

Eric knew those options were limited. Barisia and Josue would have better opportunities here. He handed her a tissue and asked what he could do to help. She hugged him tightly, clothed in just her robe and thin PJs. He pulled away when he realized what it could look like to someone on the outside and even how vulnerable she was. She needed to be with another female, not a male.

Knowing it wasn't a good time to kick her out, Eric made a joke. "So tell the truth. My wife-to-be kicked your butt, right?"

Barisia quickly recovered her real B-attitude. "As if… She's got more bark than bite." They both laughed, but Barisia immediately apologized. "I'm sorry. I answered the door in my robe. When she left, I started thinking, what if this was Josue's apartment and I was in her place? Even our friends at church cautioned me this was a bad idea. But it was different when you weren't here. So I called Mother Hernandez and she agreed to let me stay in the basement apartment at her house. It's furnished with a kitchenette. I can stay there until…"

Her voice drifted away. Then she changed the subject. "Eric, I, uh, one more thing. While I was trying to explain to Brinly why I was here I told her about you losing your job. Sorry."

Eric couldn't be mad at Barisia, especially now. It was his fault for trying to piece together a nice story for Brinly all neatly packaged, not realizing every step, every decision, was about their story and both had a role to play in it. He thought again about the wise words from his college coach and former boss: "Play your role. Play your position."

Telling Eric about how Brinly had stormed out and then broke her heel, Barisia let out a giggle. Eric laughed, too, getting a mental picture. He knew Brinly could be sensitive, but for the first time, he heard Brinly's jealous streak. That could be ugly. Lord, he prayed silently, I know she is the one, but please get rid of that.

Eric recalled how years earlier he had committed himself to memorizing 1 Corinthians 13. The line he loved most was, "Love is not jealous, it is not puffed up." But as he went to sleep God reminded him, "Love rejoices in truth." He had lied to Brinly by not coming forth about the truth of what was going on in his life. Eric hadn't set the atmosphere for truth.

Back to Brinly, learning to forgive

It was the hardest week for Brinly. She was emotionally drained from the debacle at Eric's apartment and feeling he had lied to her for three months. She returned to work to find her partner, Mr. Lockhart, involving her in yet another huge merger making the company bi-coastal. She had ten new clients to meet and she had no new ideas. She'd have to rehash designs she had done before.

Physically, Brinly was exhausted from the long flight and jumping immediately into working ten and twelve-hour days. She actually skipped church her first and second Sundays back in town to get a little more rest. And she was mad at Eric, and at herself.

She called Serena and Jackie together on a conference call. "Serena, meet my friend Jackie. Jackie, meet my friend Serena. I've decided it's time to get you two together. I'm going to tell you this, and I don't want to repeat it. Can you both get on Skype with me in about 15 minutes?"

Given her friends' busy schedules, she was surprised they both agreed immediately. Brinly opened her laptop. Always on top of things, Serena was already calling her. She accepted, then added Jackie. Both ladies cued, "Brinly and Eric are engaged at last!"

Brinly didn't know how much she liked the sound of that until she heard it out loud for the first time. "Wow, uh, no, I wish…but…" Brinly downloaded everything from the heel embarrassment to the lie-by-omission about the female roommate and the job loss until she felt a release.

Jackie, always so wise, responded first. "K, so when you finally talked to Eric, did he apologize?"

Serena didn't let Brinly respond. "Brinly, didn't I tell you men don't just throw out details? You have to wait for them to open up. I know Eric didn't mean to hurt you or lie to you."

"Did getting married make you two lose your 'how to check a man card'?" Brinly quipped.

Serena spouted back, "Brinly, you got to get a man to check him."

Ouch! That hit Brinly where it hurt.

"Eric is not officially your fiancé or husband," Serena continued. "He doesn't have to tell you anything. Furthermore, when you do have one, you have got to learn to pray for him so God will reveal all you need to know even before he does. Then you can respond appropriately, if at all. Now, Eric wasn't right, but you have to admit you can get upset easily. I don't think Skype was the best way to tell you he had a female roommate, especially with this being the first consecutive three months you guys have been in communication in over three years." Then she went there, with Proverbs 31 as her guide. "Brinly, remember you always talked about wanting to be a virtuous woman. Well, the first characteristic of that woman was her husband's trust in her. Listen to yourself. You got jealous so easily. That's not love. And that's why you were jealous because Eric trusted another woman with the details of his life more than you. Is that really his fault or something you need to own?"

She was right, of course, but it would take Brinly a bit to process that.

"You know how Justin was when I met him," Serena said. "I had every reason to suspect him of being a cheater after we got married, but at some point I realized what I feared more was what would happen if I didn't let it go."

Brinly felt like a kid on time out. "You know, this really hurts. Especially since it is true." She sighed. "I really have had trust issues for a long time. I can't take that into marriage."

Marriage. It felt now more than ever as if she was getting close to marriage—she hoped to Eric—but had she ruined her chance?

Serena switched the subject. "B, when are you going to switch your cell back to taking incoming calls? You've been back a week now."

Just then Brinly remembered she hadn't done that yet. Eric might be thinking she'd done that just to block him.

"Oops! I forgot. I need to go take care of that. Jackie and Serena, thanks for being my wise counselors. Any other advice?"

Jackie immediately interjected, "When you get married you can't talk about your husband in a negative way to anyone! Not me, not Serena, and especially not your mom. Actually, don't wait until you get married. Start now. Don't call Eric a liar. That is not his permanent character trait. Don't destroy what you're trying to build or open the door for more confusion."

"And not just the negative stuff," Serena added. "Really, treat your marriage as the holiest of holies, a place only God can touch."

Brinly was quiet, but despite all the rebukes, she was shouting on the inside. Was it really her season to be married? She had never had discussions like this with anyone before.

"Brin, I went a bit deeper than I intended with that holiest of holies reference. Are you okay?" Serena said to fill the awkward silence. "You know how to change your phone to accept incoming calls?"

Brinly began to laugh. "You know, I've gotten used to Skyping everyone and work has been so crazy there hasn't been time to think about my phone settings, let alone change them."

"So does Eric have your house phone?" Jackie wondered.

"No," Brinly answered. "We've always Skyped."

She clicked to the thread of messages she and Eric had exchanged while she was in Chile and saw one new message sent the day she came home. "My Sweet & Sassy Brinly, I'm going to miss talking to you this weekend because I've been called to "Choose Ye the Right Fast." Can't wait until you get home. We have a lot to talk about!"

Eric? Fasting? That was rare. He had told her he had only done that once a year with his church. Now she knew for sure this man was serious. Jackie was right; they needed to talk.

"Brinly, are you there?" Jackie asked. "You disappeared.

You didn't even say good-bye. Serena had to jump off."

"Oh, sorry," Brinly responded. "I was distracted for a second. I saw Eric had left me a message on Skype over a week ago when I first got back from Chile."

"And?" Jackie prodded.

Brinly coyly responded, "And as my two loving friends have advised, I'll keep this for me and Eric. But just know I think everything will be alright. We just need to talk ASAP. So I'll talk to you later."

Drawing a deep breath, Brinly called Eric's cell from her house phone. No answer. She left a quick message and asked that he call her soon so they could talk about everything. Then she picked up her cell phone and called her carrier to get her phone completely restored with domestic settings. Next there was another hard call to make.

Her first week back to work had been a complete disaster. She was so inundated by meetings, jumping into the middle of projects that had already be in the works for months, she felt lost. Her partner was trying to merge with a company on the East Coast. It was all too much after being on the mission field for five months.

Mr. Lockhart sounded surprised but pleased to hear from Brinly so late on a Sunday evening. "Hey there, Ms. Daniels. Ready for a 7am conference call with the company in D.C.?"

Whoops! Brinly had forgotten about it. That's another issue taking on this new work. It meant confusion with eastern/pacific time zone schedules.

"Mr. Lockhart—" Brinly hesitated, not sure what to say. "Uh, that's one of the reasons I called. The meetings, jumping in on projects halfway to building code inspections, it's been sort of overkill after my trip back. I've got some personal things I need to work on before I get back up to speed at work. So uh—" It was really hard for Brinly to admit she was overwhelmed.

"You are an amazing young lady, Brinly, and I know you like to give everything you do one hundred percent. It's okay if you want to take a few more days before you come back to work."

Brinly let out a breath as if she'd been holding it, relieved that he seemed to understand.

"Besides," he continued, "the staff couldn't believe you just got off your flight and came back to work the way you did and put in a full 60-hour week. How about just coming in

Monday through Wednesday?"

Thankful but needing more, she pushed even harder. "Mr. Lockhart, I'll call in on the conference call in the morning, but after that I'm taking the whole week off."

Mr. Lockhart laughed. "Ms. Daniels, for the first time, I think I've got my partner back. Ten years ago you've worked for me, but you aren't my employee anymore. I need my partner's mind at work, not just her presence."

"Thanks, Mr. Lockhart. I'll be back next Monday, sharp and ready to go. I promise."

They hung up. Brinly hoped she could deliver on her promise. It just seemed that designing offices and gutting old buildings for anonymous people who were doing it to resell later was not that exciting to her anymore. She'd rather be teaching kids or doing something she felt brought more immediate rewards.

She was drifted off to sleep when her house phone rang. She grabbed it without looking at the caller ID.

"Hello, Brinly. Welcome back."

Recognizing the voice she longed to hear every morning for

the rest of her life, Brinly's heart pounded fast and hard. Her words tumbled out. "Eric, I'm so sorry about your job. I'm sorry I popped over to your house. I'm sorry…"

Before she could finish Eric cut her off. "Brinly, wait. First, I owe you an apology. I should have shared with you from the start what was going on here. It's just hard for me to…"

"I know. I need to learn to open up. And I've got to let you talk."

"Let me finish, woman!" Eric teased. "I just want you to know I apologize. And I now know the price of lack of communication, how it can injure us, and I don't want to do that again."

He'd said "us." There's an "us!" Brinly thought. Her heart skipped a beat.

"Eric?"

"Yes, Brinly?" Eric laughed. "You can go ahead now."

Brinly began to stutter, "Uh—um, the reason I didn't call—I believed your friend Barisia—well, I've got trust issues. When I got to your place it just awakened things I had gone through in the past with men and I just can't go through that stuff again, especially not with you. So I got jealous, and I know that's not a sign of true love, but I'm committed to working on it, if you will just be patient with me."

Brinly hoped it pleased him that she could admit her own faults. He surprised her with his next words. "You got your Bible near you?"

It was under her pillow. She reached to turn on the lamp beside her bed. She sat up and opened it.

"Turn to 1 Corinthians 13," Eric said. He began to read. After he finished there was complete silence on both ends of the phone as each realized the words were written to not just hold someone else accountable, but themselves first.

Eric took the lead. "Brinly Marie Daniels, I am committed to learning to love you God's way. Now will you let me take you to breakfast? I have more to share, but not over the phone."

Eager to hear more, Brinly answered, "Shall we meet tomorrow?"

Eric surprised her by saying "No, actually I was hoping Thursday morning would work. I'll be by to pick you up at 7am and I'll have you to work by nine at the latest. Will that be alright?

"Actually, Eric, I took off work the whole week, so anytime is fine."

She thought that update might change Eric's mind, but being a man with a plan, he replied, "I'll pick you up Thursday morning seven on the dot, okay?"

They said goodnight. Filled with thoughts of Eric and their future, Brinly drifted into sleep without setting her alarm for the conference call the next morning.

Awakened at 8am to her house phone and cell phone both ringing, Brinly realized she had missed the merger kick-off discussion call. She apologized profusely to her partner. He seemed unresponsive, not the same understanding person from the day before.

She shook off her feelings of failure and decided to make the first three days of her time off all about herself. She had secretly hoped since Eric was not working they would have a blissful week, spending every day together. But she'd received the clear message last night that they wouldn't see each other until Thursday. So what was a girl to do with all that free time?

Brinly read the book of Esther and was inspired to treat herself to some spa time and special prayer preparation for her meeting with Eric.

Day One: Brinly set out to find a spa package that included massage, manicure, pedicure, and facial. She spent $500, including the tip, for one afternoon of relaxation. She rarely did something like that, but she enjoyed it.

Day Two: She spent the morning getting her hair highlighted. Then she met Serena for lunch. To her surprise, Serena didn't ask about Eric, and Brinly didn't feel the need to share their Thursday breakfast plans. The friends spent the afternoon doing what they did best together—shopping all around town—until Serena had to leave to pick up JJ from daycare.

Day Three: Brinly decided to do something she hadn't done in over two weeks—which was rare for her—write in her journal. She sat at the desk in her bedroom and began to record thoughts from her first weeks back. Then she read 1 Corinthians 13 again and realized when Eric had shared what he was committed to doing, she hadn't shared her commitment. She picked up her cell and sent him a quick text.

"Eric Shawn Washington, I'm committed to loving you God's way."

A few seconds later a text came through. "Are you sure?"

"Yes!!!" she replied.

"Good. See you in the morning."

That night Brinly once again forgot to set her alarm, but she didn't need one. Promptly at five o'clock in the morning she awakened as God ushered her into prayer. She prayed for family, friends, her children back in Chile, her church, her business with Mr. Lockhart and then she began to pray for her future.

When she finished praying, God led her to study Genesis. She noted that when Abraham had received the call to "Go," it was not to go to a specific place. It was simply, "Go to a place I will show you."

As Brinly put her thoughts into her journal, she realized God was calling her to "Go" without telling her when or where. Would it be with Eric?

Her phone began to ring, signaling the end of her prayer time. Eric was en route. Uh-oh. Thankfully, Brinly had laid out her blue sundress with teal trim the night before. She jumped into the shower and then into her clothes. The doorbell rang before she'd put on her jewelry or makeup. She went to the door in her dress and shower shoes. What a look!

When she opened it no one was there. Looking down, she saw an Edible Arrangement. Brinly picked it up, forgetting to close the door, and took it to the table in the kitchen. Turning to close the door, she almost jumped out of her skin.

Eric stood in the living room holding roses in one hand and a box of her favorite pastries in the other. A Starbucks coffee carrier sat on the end table—all her favorite things for breakfast provided by her favorite man. He was dressed casually in a sweat suit looking like he was ready to play basketball, an odd look for breakfast outing, she thought.

"I was hoping we could eat in," Eric said. "Then we can talk before...."

Brinly waited, for once realizing this man needed some time to get his words out.

Eric concluded, "I only want to get married one time."

Brinly smiled. "Me too."

"I want you to agree to go through this pre-marital counseling with me. I know we both want to learn to love each other God's way so I invited Table for 1 relationship counselors to your house. They will be here at 8 o'clock so we can eat breakfast, talk and then have our first session. Okay?" He paused nervously. "I mean, if this is too much... I know I should have asked first before inviting people to your house, but ..."

"Well..." Brinly paused. "...I guess we need this counseling more than I originally thought." She laughed at his tension. "Eric, this is fine. I told you I'm committed and I'm glad you are, too."

Brinly felt overjoyed. She couldn't believe Eric had taken the initiative to schedule this for them. She was so excited. She couldn't believe she wasn't worried about a ring or an official proposal. None of that mattered. She was confident, not in Eric, but in Christ. This was indeed what He had designed her for and she wouldn't let official titles, rings or wedding dates ruin the journey God had for her and Eric together.

Eric stepped forward to place the pastry box on the table. Brinly grabbed his hand. They hadn't even hugged. Eric drew her close and began to kiss her gently all over her face. It felt good, but Brinly backed away. She grabbed the throw cover from the couch and laid it out on the living room floor. Eric looked perplexed. She was amused, knowing what he was thinking. Had she gotten the wrong signals? Didn't she know Christian marital counselors would be there within the hour?

"Bring the Edible Arrangement and the pastries," she said grinning. "Let's have a breakfast picnic."

Eric swallowed visibly. "Sure. I was hoping I didn't have to tell you not to touch the jewels."

They both laughed.

The hour went by too fast. Eric told her more about Table for 1, how they are based on the East Coast but have a few field counselors out West and how his mom and his best friend had used them prior to getting married. Wow! Eric had done his research.

Later, Eric brought her up to date on how his job search had been going. He hinted that he had a new career plan, but wanted to share more about it when he was ready. Brinly began to wonder if Eric could afford this Table for 1 program and offered to help pay. But he immediately assured her his old job would pay for counseling as a part of his separation package.

They had cleaned up the food and were talking at the kitchen table. Brinly shared with Eric how she had lost the passion for her job since her return. Just as Eric was giving her some advice, the doorbell rang.

Brinly asked Eric to get the door since he knew the counselors. To be a good hostess, she prepared a pitcher of water and glasses for the meeting.

Eric welcomed the counselors, a couple which had been married for twenty-three years named Sam and Karen Rawlings. They finished each other's sentences. Brinly and Eric felt comfortable with them. They asked how long Brinly and Eric had been together.

"Three years," Brinly replied.

At the same time Eric said, "Three months."

Sam and Karen looked confused.

Brinly rattled off an abbreviated version of their journey together. The couple laughed and Karen said, "Really, you two should have been married two years ago."

"Actually, we weren't ready," Brinly said. "The right person at the wrong time is still wrong."

Sam applauded Brinly's ability to understand that. He chided his wife, saying she relied on Romans 8:28 when it came to marriage, trusting God to work it all out.

Eric seemed quiet at first, letting Brinly defend their relationship. The session with the Rawlings was a breakthrough for them both. The counselors immediately drilled in on the real issues. Karen asked what areas they each thought they needed to focus on as individuals to be a stronger couple.

Immediately, Eric confessed, "I tend to omit some things to avoid conflict and don't communicate everything as I should."

Brinly admitted, "I'm no spring chicken about to get married. I've been through a lot and I tend to have trust issues and become jealous easily."

Eric put his arm around Brinly has she shared to let her know he understood. The counselors reassured them that their sessions would help them deal with these matters at the root of their relationship.

"You two are more alike than you think," Sam said. "Eric, when you omit the truth, and Brinly, when you get jealous, although they look different, the root cause is the same— PRIDE."

Karen supported her husband's statement. "Yes, we all have to get to the spiritual root of our actions. We have to kill it from the root so it won't produce a harvest of bitter fruit. You both are battling issues with pride. And you two know the Word. Pride goes before a fall, and God hates pride."

Sam gave them an activity called IntoMESEE. "Eric, hold Brinly's hands, look into her eyes, and tell her something you've never shared with her before that makes you feel exposed."

Brinly could tell Eric didn't want to go first, but he was the man, and he needed to take the lead. So he looked into her eyes. "Well, a long time ago...." Eric shared about how he almost went to the NBA and how his injury literally changed his life. He told her he thought she was so beautiful, not just on the outside, but on the inside, too, and that he didn't know why it took him so long to open up to her.

Brinly began to cry, remembering all the times she'd thought Eric had such an arrogant walk and didn't know he had a metal knee. Eric's fingers traced Brinly's face and dried the tears she shed for him.

When it was Brinly's turn, she looked directly into Eric's eyes, probably for the first time since she'd known him. She shared how she had lost her virginity in a date rape. Because she hadn't been bold enough to say what she believed and stand on it, she had given in and, in many ways, had been fighting ever since.

Like producers on a reality TV show, Sam and Karen watched these exchanges nodding their heads encouragingly. The hour-long session ended so quickly. They agreed to meet next time at Eric's house a month later.

Brinly cringed, thinking about his roommate situation. But Eric seemed to sense her thoughts and whispered, "She moved out last week."

"What was that?" Sam asked.

"Nothing," Eric and Brinly replied together.

The Rawlings left them a homework assignment to do a Hebrew Word study on "pride" and try to do one "IntoMESee" activity each week. They cautioned that the more "IntoMe" activities they completed the more their desire for intimacy would increase so they should try to do them by phone and not in-person.

Eric walked the counselors to the elevator then returned to tell Brinly he had to leave because he was working on something for them that he would share later that night. He asked if they could have dinner together.

"How about we order in?" Brinly asked, concerned about his finances.

"Woman, you are going to learn, you are so beautiful I want to take you out. I didn't get to do it this morning, but I will tonight. Promise." He kissed her on the nose and was out the door in a moment.

Brinly dropped onto the couch just filled with bliss and wanting to share with her girls. But this was just about her and Eric now. No need to share anything. They would know when they got their wedding invitations. Invitations? Brinly laughed. She still didn't even have a ring.

She decided to take a nap and then call her family in Chicago. Her twin brothers were in their last year of medical school. She couldn't believe how time had flown by. One was engaged and the other—let's just say needed prayer. Her dad was busy working at the university and her mom, as usual, stayed faithful to supporting everyone but herself.

Brinly went ahead and told her mom about her courtship with Eric. Her mom screamed with joy so that Brinly's ear was ringing. But Brinly asked her mom to wait to tell her father when it was closer to his meeting Eric. Her dad's first question was going to be, "Can he provide for you?" and with Eric's current situation this was definitely not a good time to bring her dad up to speed.

Later, when Eric picked her up for dinner, Brinly was pleasantly surprised to see Eric dressed out of a men's fashion magazine. She wasn't quite ready for this upscale look in just a sundress. She had to change so as not to be outdone by her man. They went to their favorite seafood restaurant. For dessert he surprised her with Justin and Serena joining them. It was very reminiscent of when they'd connected years before. Serena hugged Brinly good-bye, and whispered in her ear, "Let it flow. Enjoy the journey."

Brinly smiled. She was indeed enjoying the journey.

Three months passed. Brinly was ecstatic with her home life, but was miserable at work. In fact, the only thing she enjoyed about workdays were her once-a-week lunch getaways with Eric. She tried to volunteer with the youth at church, but she was feeling pulled as she had to make time for Eric and her courtship homework and pre-marital counseling.

She also worried that Eric still had not found work and he wouldn't let her pay for anything. Was that a pride issue? she wondered. The courtship journey was more work than she'd initially anticipated and the growing intimacy made it more difficult. To make sure they didn't start anything they weren't prepared to finish, Eric even said no more hugs and kisses.

She brought it up at one of their counseling sessions. Eric just about flipped his lid. Sam had to calm him down. Brinly had not seen Eric so upset since the mission field. She was turned completely OFF.

Then Eric did something that shocked Brinly. He pulled a blue velvet box from his pants pocket. "I've been walking around with this ring," he said to the counselors. "I designed it for Brinly to give her when she first got back from Chile. To be the head she needs me to be, I've been waiting for the right time to propose. But it's like I don't get any breathing room. Brinly wants to know everything. Especially when it comes to money. I can't propose to her knowing that God has shown me all the details. All I know is I'll be starting my own business and we might need to move to another city. But Brinly needs to know when, where, how and I just can't propose knowing I don't know yet."

While Brinly's jaw dropped at Eric's outburst, Karen and Sam just smiled. "Now we're getting somewhere," Sam said. "Eric, we were going to confront you and Brinly about an ultimatum date—the day you guys decide to end your courtship and be engaged, or maybe decide you were not meant to be and walk away."

"All we can do is counsel and support," Karen said, "but ultimately you two have to be confident God has joined you together for such a time as this to be husband and wife."

Brinly humbled herself. "Eric, I'm sorry I make you feel you have to know all the details laid out for us all the time. You should know if anyone would support your vision to be an entrepreneur it would be me."

That session happened to be at Eric's house. While he went to his bedroom for a moment, Sam and Karen educated Brinly briefly on what it meant for the man to be the provider, providing vision, not just money. They also explained how she and Eric needed to agree about roles concerning money upfront, and that every household is different. She could not try to apply her mom's and dad's model to her union with Eric.

Brinly nodded, silently repenting for trying to make Eric fit the mold of how her dad is with her mom. Just then, Eric walked back in looking shy as he held a white board covered with words and visuals cut from magazines.

This man has a vision board, Brinly thought, smiling. He is full of surprises.

Eric was about to start his presentation when Sam interrupted. "This is just for you and Brinly. Karen and I will leave now. We will expect a full report later. And keep up the IntoMeSEE work."

Wait, don't go, Brinly thought. She was now totally turned back ON. But after they were gone she focused herself to listen and hear the voice of God, not the gorgeous man she wished she belonged to that very night.

So Eric shared the vision God had given him since he'd been laid off from work.

Eric's Vision Board:

Washington Learning Center

An online school for at-risk students to finish high school and an afterschool program for middle school children. He had started working on obtaining a 501c3, he was researching grants, and he was looking at buildings in San Francisco as well as Brinly's hometown of Chicago and his hometown in Maryland, cautious to let God establish the plans for this vision.

"Eric, I love you, and I love this vision," Brinly said. Realizing to be involved she would need to relinquish some of her duties at the firm, she continued, "I'd even love to design the center. And I could help teach in the evening hours."

Eric grinned. He set the board aside and got down on one

knee in front of her. "Brinly Marie Daniels, will you marry me?"

Brinly only nodded and held out her hand. Eric slipped a platinum diamond-encrusted band with a 1.5 carat pear-shaped diamond on her finger. He kissed her on the lips for the first time since before their first counseling session. "I'm never letting you go," he whispered.

They sat on the couch the rest of that Saturday afternoon enjoying being in each other's presence. No vision plans, no "IntoMeSEE" questions. They simply enjoyed being in each other's presence.

They spent the rest of the weekend together just doing silly, fun things. They took a trolley around San Francisco and a speed boat around Fisherman's Wharf. They only parted to sleep. Now that the commitment was made it seemed the intensity about unwrapping their gifts for one another before the honeymoon subsided.

It was actually two weeks before Brinly had a chance to share the engagement with her friends. She didn't wear her ring to work the first two weeks, just enjoying the private commitment she and Eric shared. Ever conscious of the budget, which Eric began to appreciate as they investigated wedding costs, Brinly decided to use a free community festival as the perfect time to invite her friends and Eric's, most of whom still lived in San Diego, to share their announcement.

Brinly met Eric's old roommates, a really odd bunch, but fun nonetheless. While Eric already knew Justin and Serena, he met Brinly's old mentee and her daughter and her employees. Although he had seen her partner a time or two, he got to talk to him in more detail. Eric was proud of the woman he was marrying.

Driving home afterward, Brinly said, "I want to go."

"Go where?" Eric asked. "I'm taking you home. It's late and we don't want to get caught up in anything."

Brinly laughed. "I'm praying for your mind, Eric. I meant 'go.' I want to leave. I'm ready to leave San Francisco, and I remember your vision board. I was just wondering if you would hear me out."

"I set the lead," Eric answered soberly, "but B, I'm always open for your input. Tell me what you are talking about."

"Well, you know I haven't been happy at work. I'm thinking about divesting from the company and using that money to pay for our wedding and for starting the business. But I was thinking, maybe God wants us to start it somewhere else."

Eric grabbed her hand, driving with the other. "You are so sweet. I just don't want you to use your money to invest. What if it fails?"

"There is no failure in God. We will soon be one. I have to invest in every way into Washington Learning Center."

Eric squeezed her hand. "Let's pray about it. I have been thinking about going back home to Maryland. You know they could really use this in my old neighborhood."

The reality of what Brinly had just said sank in. Maryland? She'd never even visited Maryland. She was thinking more like the south or sticking with someplace warm. But back to the "cold?" She agreed to pray for real.

Karen and Sam had voice mailed them reminding them it would be important to visit both families for the coming holidays. So weeks later, Brinly sat in Maryland at Eric's aunt's apartment with her future in-laws around the table, including her twelve-year-old future brother in-law. Eric's stepfather seemed nice, and his mother was cautious but pleasant as well. Of course Christina, Eric's cousin, remembered Brinly from one of her visits to the West Coasts and they had a great time together.

Eric was distracted. He couldn't believe how this old building had never been renovated. The crown molding was cracked. There was a new kitchen sink and refrigerator but the floor made so much noise. The doorways were way too small and with the borrowed tables that had been put together filling the space, there was really no place they could all relax together.

Everyone decided to go to the movies together after dinner. Brinly knew from her mother's etiquette training you should not leave someone's house without saying something nice, so she complimented the wonderful furniture in the living room, which had been recently purchased by Christina for her mom.

As Eric's immediate family stood up leave, her future little brother squeezed her around her hips and she returned the hug. Her future mother in-law suggested she call her some time, which was a shock to Brinly since she'd barely said three words to her. And Coach Frank, Eric's stepdad, was the best. He told her to keep Eric in line. Brinly offered to help Eric's aunt clean up, but the hostess graciously refused the help. So Brinly and Eric got ready to return to their hotel to rest up for the first flight out to Chicago in the morning to visit Brinly's clan.

Christina reached for her purse, which was so big Brinly could have fit four of hers in it. From one of those designers

Brinly could never allow herself to support, it had jewels and charms all over it. Christina reached inside and drew out an envelope. Handing it to Brinly, she said, "Here is your engagement present."

Brinly handed it to Eric to open. It was a deed, a deed to the building, the building where Eric and Christina had grown up, the same crammed place where they had all struggled to enjoy their family dinner.

What?

Christina said, "Look, Brinly, I don't know how much Eric has told you about this building or this neighborhood, but it was his paternal grandfather's building that was lost to a slum lord. But when he died I had the chance to buy it, and I did. I bought it at an auction. It was a steal. So I wanted to give it back to Eric to have something that connects him to the Washington family legacy."

"What legacy?" Eric said bitterly. "A legacy of leaving?" Brinly knew he was referring to his father.

He tossed the deed on the table nearby. "It's time to go," he said.

Secretly, Brinly felt relieved. The building needed a lot of repair work, and they definitely weren't moving to Maryland, especially to this building. She supported her husband-to-be. She said, "Thanks, Christina. Really, thanks. But I don't think it's for us."

"Just pray about it," Christina pleaded. "My mom's new condo will be ready in the spring. Let me know by then if you want it, or I will sell it to someone else." She placed the deed in Brinly's hand.

Brinly took the deed and stuffed it into her purse. She hated to leave like that, but she knew Eric well enough to know it was time to go.

After Eric hugged his aunt good-bye, Brinly led him gracefully by her pinky finger in his hand to make sure he was forced to hug Christina good-bye.

Eric was moody as he drove the car rental back to the hotel. This was the first time they would be sharing the same room together. They each secretly worried temptation might rise up again, but thanks to Eric's temper, the hotel room would be safe. When Eric prayed that night Brinly was not invited to join him. With stale good nights, Brinly went to her bed and Eric went to his.

The next morning they rushed to turn in their rental car and head to Chicago. Brinly prayed silently that Garrett's Popcorn would be open when they arrived in the airport. Eric could kill her sexual desires, but nothing could kill her craving for sweet caramel and cheddar popcorn. Ah! She smelled it as soon as they entered the terminal. Garrett's was indeed open; one temptation would be indulged that weekend.

In Chicago, there was no need for a rental car or hotel. Brinly's dad had the visit all planned under his watchful eye. Mr. Daniels picked up the future newlyweds. It was quite uncomfortable for Brinly. Eric and her dad exchanged four words—woops, make that eight—on the ride from O'Hare to the south suburbs.

"Good flight?"

"Yes sir. Thanks for the ride."

So Brinly rattled on and on about how much food they'd had at Eric's aunt's—not that it was as good as her mom's—but it was a lot of food.

Fortunately, Brinly's extended family had come over the day before. So when they go to the house it was just Brinly, Eric and her parents with time alone to get know one another.

"So, Eric, what do you do again?" Mr. Daniels asked. "IT or something, right?"

"Actually, I was working for a software development company but was laid off about six months ago," Eric answered honestly.

"Well, it's good you two haven't set a wedding date yet then. You waiting to get a job? That's wise."

Brinly held her breath as she prayed, Lord, no. Please don't let Eric go off on my daddy. That would be a deal breaker.

"Actually," Eric said, "we haven't set a date yet because God hasn't shown us the timing. And as far as the job, I'm not looking for one."

Now Brinly held her breath praying, Lord, please don't let my daddy go off on Eric, telling him no man without a job is marrying his daughter.

"Then, young man, you must have a plan."

"Yes, sir."

End of discussion.

Brinly was shocked and amazed, amazed and shocked. What would come next? Why did she have to ask?

"Do you want to be a father one day?" Mrs. Daniels asked.

"Yes, of course," Eric replied.

Please, Mom, no! Brinly thought. Not the "Brinly's eggs are dying every day" talk!

So Brinly interrupted. "Mom, weren't you in your late thirties when you had the twins? And Eric's mom had his little brother when she was in her early forties. So we're in good company getting a late start."

Brinly's mom looked scared, like why on earth would anyone do that? Just then the doorbell rang. Ding dong. Thank God! Speaking of the twins, it was Brinly's brothers, Darren and Darryl, just in time. Brinly didn't know if Eric appreciated her running interference for him, but she gave a hopeful sigh of relief.

Fortunately, the twins lightened the mood for everyone. Eric couldn't believe how much Brinly was like her brothers. Although, they were a lot taller, they all loved to chat it up. And all three kids had the same hazel eyes from Brinly's father.

While they were in Chicago, Brinly didn't get a moment to talk to Eric about his family's gathering or the engagement gift. On their flight back to San Francisco she had the courage to bring it up.

"Just enjoy the flight and go to sleep," Eric told her. He closed his eyes and soon began deep, even breathing.

She was tired, so she slept, too. When she woke she went into her purse to look for some gum and saw the deed Christina had given them. She took a closer look. It wasn't just for the house, but for some land around it, enough space for Washington Learning Center. She knew Eric wanted to do something good for his community—whether Eric liked to admit it or not—something good for the Washington family legacy. Brinly decided not to mention all this, just to pray about it.

The next weeks went by in a blur. Christmas came and went. They'd decided instead of giving one another gifts they would buy gifts together as a couple for their parents. They even surprised their premarital counselors, Sam and Karen, with a gift.

The Rawlings officially ended their pre-marital counseling sessions, telling them they wished more couples would focus on planning a lifetime of marriage not just a wedding day. But they also urged them to set a date saying, "You don't want to leave the door open for temptation."

Eric remembered all too well what he had been through and didn't want that again, but he also didn't want to move ahead of God. He had a lifetime memory of that in his knee. Brinly heard their counselors well and asked Eric if they could fast until the New Year arrived.

It wasn't just about setting a wedding date. Brinly had finally decided to do something about her lack of interest and passion for her career. She told Eric about resigning at the beginning of the year. Eric said if she'd prayed about her decision he would fully support her. So there they were on New Year's Eve with a vision, but no jobs, and with a wedding to plan.

They had decided to go to Brinly's church that night. The Sermon topic? "Is God Pro Your Vision?" As Eric listened, he kept hearing that this season of his life was not just about waiting on God, but about moving in faith, knowing if God had given this vision He would provide for it. He then recalled a lesson he had learned about the wife being a man's favor. Eric needed Brinly as his wife now more than ever. In fact, they needed each other.

Eric reflected on the first time he caught a glimpse of his angel Brinly at this same church almost four years ago. Then, when he was realized she was the "one" was in Chile. Both times took place in July. Knowing Brinly would know the exact date and time for Chile, he whispered, "Let's get married in July."

True to form, Brinly said, "How about July 14th? That's the day…"

Eric laughed, "I knew you would know the date and know why I had picked July. I love you."

They would have kissed, but it was almost midnight and the pastor was asking everyone to get on their knees and pray in the New Year. Brinly and Eric held hands as they prayed.

Eric made an entry on his Lone Wolf blog, but for the first time he felt comfortable making it with Brinly hanging out at his house. She sat reading on the other side of the room. He thought about the Proverbs 31 virtuous woman scripture, the part where it says the husband's heart "safely trusts" in her. Eric knew he could trust Brinly with every part of his life. He felt bad he had ever hidden anything from her.

Tonight he entitled his blog "The Fearless Vision"

Fearlessly called to fulfill an impossible vision
Eager to see the kind God alone gives without repentance.
Allowing the Holy Spirit to fill in details, order steps and keep pace.
Realizing we can't do this alone, God sends a partner and mate.
Loving without fear, natural eyes wide shut, on faith alone we stand. Even the Word without love leaves us powerless, like an empty hand.
Surrendering to Godfor sustainable power and provision.
Submitting to His will, not our own, becomes our sole mission.

Eric realized this new vision was not new to God and he should see it not as a burden to carry or something to hide from, but as a treasure to be cherished and to be stewarded, not just for himself, but for his and Brinly's future. So his "I's", became "we" and the rest is for you to read and see.

Part V: The Spoon

*"Scoop the Desires
of Your Heart"*

S o, here I am still single, writing this second book four years after the first. The Bible says in Psalm 37:4: "Delight thyself in the Lord and you shall receive the desires of your heart." Am I not married because I haven't delighted myself in the Lord? No. The word "desire" in the Old Testament was originally written as the Hebrew word, "mishalots." This word can be translated as "exquisite delicacy." When a person is focused and yielding totally to celebrating God in their life, the mishalots line up with His divine will and are pleasing to the Lord.

Now, how do I answer why I am still single? I don't blame God, or myself, but my "mishalots," or as I call them, things I "miss a lot." God knows me better than I do. Whether I like to admit it or not at the core of my heart, my "mishalots" were not for marriage. They have been for living on purpose and helping others do the same, and sometimes forgetting or even avoiding my own self. Why? I'm setting the table for one for God to reveal and heal that too. Told you, I'm imperfect. God has been preparing me for the perfect imperfect person just for me.

Let's talk about timing. It's not about age, but about the wisdom you will need to get married and stay married. Or maybe, just maybe, you or your spouse have been out of position to receive one another. Whatever it is, I urge you—if you are single, don't blame God, your future spouse, or the ex, but focus totally on the King of kings and Lord of lords.

Trust me, I know this single-and-whole walk is indeed hard to live out, especially when both the world and the church, when you are in a relationship or married, say things like these: "I just want you to be happy." Or "I'm glad you found someone to make you happy."

Interestingly, I've also heard people before or after getting a divorce say things such as, "I just wanted to be happy." So which is it? I actually tear up when people close to me ask, "Are you happy?" I cry because I realize how much they really don't know me, or know who I live to please.

Because I know who I am in Christ, I am filled with unspeakable JOY. I know without a shadow of doubt I am living life on-purpose and can live in victory every day for the rest of my life. It all comes down to who I am trying to please – me or God? I'd like to believe God.

Trust me, I can imagine for many of you reading this book it was a struggle to even purchase a book with a title about a table for one. So I ask you: What are your "mishalots?" Or should I say, what are the things you "miss a lot" that you think would bring you exquisite pleasure?

Whatever they are, I ask you to lay them at the feet of Jesus, or on the altar, and ask God to open the eyes of your heart. When you see Him, He will reveal the things and people you will "miss a lot" if you lose focus on putting Him first.

Matthew 6:33 says, *"Seek first the kingdom of God and His righteousness and all these things shall be added to you."*

This reminds me of a song with a verse that says, "This world has nothing for me." Everything we see is temporary. Our own bodies will turn back to the ground, but our souls will live for eternity. My future marriage is not about my temporary "happiness," but about the eternal reward for being faithful over what the Lord gives me on this side of life, as a single whole person, both wile unmarried and as a covenant partner in marriage.

What can I leave as a legacy to the next generation that will stand firm and endure these last days? I'm not living for the world's standard of happiness, but for the kingdom to come on earth as it is in heaven.

What does that mean? Dig into God and He will show the territories and assignments designed just for you to reclaim for his kingdom. For some this includes marriage in the near future and for others this may demand a single wholehearted attention for seasons longer than others.

Regardless of your marital status, all of us will be renewed, transformed, and experience our true "mishalots" when we settle down and dine at the table for one.

On the male side of the table, you would be amazed at the number of men I have met over the past few years who are looking for the "one" to share their table. All of them admit they have been led by the flesh and not the Spirit at times, a tendency to be picky versus open, a desire for perfection versus the perfect "imperfect" one designed just for them. Truthfully, if we are all honest, we've been there at some time in our lives.

Be encouraged, every married man I interviewed knew their wife was the "one" within the first few weeks of their initial meeting. Whether it was a fleeting thought or bonafide, "bone of my bone, flesh of my flesh" moment they knew even if they did not pursue at that time. Some men had never admitted it to their wives and thanked me for the extra points I helped them rack up. Smile! So single women, play your position, be found a wife—not as a bride, (future book coming) and single men find a wife, not a "wifey" substitute.

Finally believing singles, I must share that if you say there are no "good" options or meditate on that there will not be anyone for you. When you decide that is a lie, the eyes of your heart will be open to see all the great and mighty choices available to you. Then you must set your table for one again, asking God to help you choose wisely. While the man must be wise enough to know he has indeed found his wife, the woman must be wise in choosing if this is her "mishalot."

Now back to Eric and Brinly, as their long-awaited separate "mishalots" become one. (Introducing the beginning of Table for 1, Still?)

July was only five months away, and the year was moving fast. Brinly were clear on one thing: She and Eric were FINALLY getting married. Once they set the date July 14th it was amazing how everything sped up in their lives.

Brinly's resignation from her firm was rejected. Instead, she was offered the chance to be a consultant with the completion of the company's merger with a Maryland firm. While she and Eric were praying about that, Eric got a call from a recruiter offering him a position to consult on a government contract in D.C. for nine months.

They had started flying back and forth, spending two weeks at a time in the Maryland/D.C. area and often not on the same weeks. They had to officially make a date night to stay grounded in each other and planning the wedding. But they seemed to argue over every detail. Eric wanted a big wedding. Brinly preferred a mid-sized ceremony in her hometown. This seemed absurd to Eric since she hadn't lived in Chicago for over twenty years. He wondered, who does that?

Finally they agreed to keep the wedding intimate with only immediate family and close friends. It was already March and they hadn't picked out invitations. The wedding details were on the back burner because Brinly's mind was on the deed. So one night after work in Maryland she called Eric's aunt and asked to come by for a visit. She walked around the property and made a few assessments. She really thought this could be the future site for Eric's vision of Washington Learning Center.

Brinly was more committed to this than even finding her own wedding dress. She stayed up every night designing blueprints for a small school, a house and an afterschool program. The building had a wing for classrooms, a few offices and a play area. Brinly even researched zoning codes and laws on learning centers in the area. With this purpose driving her, Brinly regained her passion for architecture.

When she met with Eric that week she had to share these plans. It was time to give Christina a final answer. Brinly had called in a favor from an artist friend asking him to design a WLC logo for Washington Learning Center.

Eric was so busy he asked Brinly if they could meet at his house for dinner. Brinly agreed and surprised him by coming with Chinese food, a movie and her architecture briefcase with the plans for Washington Learning Center.

Brinly had learned a lot about her husband-to-be over the past year. So instead of playing with words, she was prompted to action. After dinner she took his plate and replaced it with a silver dessert platter with the deed for the property where they would build the learning center.

Still consumed by his money woes, Eric responded half-jokingly, "What's this, a pre-nup?"

Brinly laughed. "No, goofball, it's the deed—the deed to your family's property Christina gave us as an engagement present."

"You are incredible. How did you know I've been thinking about that?"

Brinly said, "I didn't. What's up?"

"I think God wants us to keep the house," he said firmly. "I mean, I loved my grandfather. Heck, he's the reason I never changed my last name. I don't think it's your style for living there, but if we are going to be spending so much of our time in the Maryland/D.C. area we need to make that our home-base and do something good with the house for the community. You know?"

Brinly sat straight up. "Agreed. Actually, I've been praying God would lead you to accept the deed."

"Why?" Eric snickered. "I know the future Mrs. is not considering living in the hood."

"Eric, I could live anywhere with you." She jumped up and grabbed her briefcase filled with the blueprints and amazed her husband-to-be yet again. This time it was Eric who was completely turned ON by his future wife's vision.

His eyes beamed with joy as Brinly chatted away about each and every detail of the plans. On the couch she spread out plans for classrooms all equipped with computers. The dining room table was filled with play areas. On the coffee table lay an outline for a couples' suite in case they needed to give someone a place to live above the school. The woman had thought of everything. Everything, that is, except security. But Eric knew they could add some things for that. And of course, God would protect his house.

Eric told her he loved it and picked her up like that first time he saw her in Chile, hugged her and kissed her ever so sweetly on her forehead, nose and then her lips. He found a resting spot on her neck and whispered, "Just one thing—does it have to be called 'Washington Learning Center'?"

Brinly was a little taken aback. "No, but I thought it was for your family's legacy."

"This is more about what God has done through us. How about 'Kingdom Learning Center'?"

Brinly loved it. After all, every child would not be a Washington, but they all would have access to the kingdom.

Knowing Eric was in a good mood, she ventured one other suggestion. "Eric, could we do a destination wedding?"

That would be more expensive than Chicago, Eric thought. Then he looked at the work his bride had done for him. "Yes, beautiful lady. Whatever you want. Just as long as I am married to you by sundown on July 14th."

"Hmm. I'm glad you said that," Brinly replied. "I was thinking, let's go back to Chile and get married."

Eric thought about the way he had left and what he had learned since. "Brinly, I know you thought this was going to be difficult, but yeah, I actually think that is a great idea.

I even wrote a letter to Senor Perez a few months ago and apologized for my behavior that day I left. I also told him we were now engaged."

"Well, if it's not too awkward, let's have him conduct our ceremony. Of course, we will be married legally still in California, and don't worry about the budget. We have friends in Chile who will support the festivities and our families can pull together to make sure everyone who needs to be there will have a flight and a hotel."

Eric, shaking his head, responded, "Well, smarty pants, you think of everything."

"Yes, I do," she grinned.

Eric winked. "I like the sound of that. But it's not quite true. You forgot one thing."

"What?"

"People with kids like Justin and Serena. And what about Jackie?"

Brinly looked sad. "Oh boy, you're right. They might not want the babies to travel over there. They are still young."

Eric, recognizing he was starting to worry Brinly unnecessarily, calmed her by concluding, "Don't worry about it. Everyone who is supposed to be there, will be there."

On July 14th, Brinly, dressed in an antique white lace off-the-shoulder gown, stood outside the small schoolhouse in Chile where Eric had taken off running just a year earlier. Her matrons of honor, Jackie and Serena, stood wearing strapless gold dinner dresses. Eric, in a nice tuxedo, wore a beautiful gold tie while his groomsmen, ex-roomies Troy and Lloyd, and his little brother wore tan suits with gold ties. Eric had picked both men on purpose, to inspire them to consider marriage one day.

The music began and their guests, a total of forty-one, including their local friends, were seated. Brinly took a deep breath and walked down the paper runner at the back of the schoolhouse. As she walked, she beamed, despite the fact that her twin brothers were escorting her instead of her father. Mr. Daniels thought Eric's plan and vision was a crazy way to start off a marriage, so he'd refused to give his only daughter to Eric. So while he showed up with Brinly's mom, he adamantly refused to walk her down the aisle. Although it hurt, Brinly focused on her future and believed in Eric's vision that the Lord had given him.

Suddenly, as she neared the spot where Senor Perez waited to perform the vows, Brinly's father stood, almost in sync with the soft music. Her brothers stopped, stepped back, and Mr. Daniels took his daughter's arm to escort her the rest of the way to the altar.

"Daddy," Brinly gasped, sounding faintly like a seven-year old little girl once again.

Mr. Daniels leaned over and kissed her on the cheek. "I just had to be sure you were ready to do this with or without my blessing," he said.

Eric grinned ear to ear as Mr. Daniels placed his bride's hand in his. Tears reddened both Brinly's and Eric's eyes.

Senor Perez raised the glass goblet and began to share its history with the wedding guests. He used it to give Eric and Brinly communion as a sign of their new covenant as "one" with each other. Eric now understood the reason for Senor Perez's anger a year before. It wasn't about the glass itself. It was the purpose for which it was to be used in his church. Only for communion. He compared that to the vows he and Brinly had written for one another. They both highlighted knowing the purpose for which they were called.

Purpose is what led them to have custom party favors for each guest.

Eric and Brinly wrote a thank you poem and had it mounted in gold frames for their guests to take home. It read"

Is Marriage My Desire?

Is marriage my desire? And he said,
To love someone more than my very own life?
To sacrificially give, even amidst adversities and strife?
Lord, help me to desire my one and only wife.

Is marriage my desire? And she said,
To love and trust this man hears from God as the head of our house?
To let go of my selfish plans, fears and doubts?
Lord, help me to desire my one and only husband and spouse.

Marriage is our desire. And they said,
To submit to God and one another with our whole hearts and pray.
To surrender our own rights, for choosing one single and whole way.
Lord, help us to desire a marriage honoring you each and every day.

After the "I do's," the music was turned up and the outdoor wedding guests enjoyed dancing, laughter and delicious food. A few times Brinly noticed her friend Serena looking a little sad. She had to excuse herself from her new husband. (Wow! She could finally call Eric her husband!)

Brinly assumed Serena was missing her little boy, Justin Jr., since it was the first time she had left him alone since he'd been born. He was at home with his dad, Justin Sr. As she approached her, Brinly thought of the many miracles God had done in her friend's life. Serena had won a battle with cancer—not once but twice—and she had prayed her ex-NFL husband, from a Sunday church-goer to a true Christ knower. Brinly grabbed Serena's glass and joked, "You got vodka in there lady? Why so teary?"

Serena seemed surprised Brinly had noticed. "Girl, get back to your husband."

"What's up, girl," Brinly persisted. "You should be shouting the most, outside of my mom, of course." They both laughed.

Thinking she knew the problem, Brinly said, "I won't be offended if you call Justin and talk to your little boy. I know this must be hard."

Floodgates opened and Serena mumbled, "I haven't talked

to Justin in weeks. Justin Jr. is at home with my aunt. It's over, it's over." She seemed to hiccup and cry at the same time.

Brinly hugged her sweet friend as if she were a little baby. She saw Eric looking through the small crowd, his eyes searching for Brinly and seeing something wrong looked really anxious. Brinly held up one finger indicating she needed a minute, or should we say a Table for one?

But Brinly didn't know Eric was looking for her not just to continue celebrating. His mom and stepfather had surprised him with a wedding gift, a letter from his biological father. A man he had never met, wrote him a letter to congratulate him on his wedding. Eric wanted to read it with his wife, but she seemed too busy comforting her friend. He thought they were now one, but somehow in that moment, holding the unopened letter he felt very much like still the lone wolf. Could it be table for one, still?

Learn more about Brinly, Eric, Justin and Serena in Table for 1, Still?—the married edition—and Table for 1, Again?—a special edition for those who find themselves single again.

HOW TO SET YOUR TABLE FOR ONE:

Resource Recommendations

Ready to set the table for one with God?

I. GLASS: Single & Whole

Do you have a personal relationship with Christ?

• Prayer & Confession

• The Holy Bible

II. KNIFE: Cut the Substitutes

Do you want God to cut the substitutes distracting you from a closer relationship at one with Him?

• Prayer

• The Holy Bible

• Any kind of habitual sin - www.settingcaptivesfree.com

• Lover of Self - The M Word By Debbie Adebayo

• Porn/Sex - www.everymanministries.com; Every Man's Battle by S. Arterburn, F. Stoeker

III. CHAIR (for the men) FORK (for the women): Spiritual Growth

Are you ready for more of God and less of you?

Top Picks for Men	**Top Picks for Women**
The Holy Bible	The Holy Bible

Man of God: Leading Your Family By Allowing God to Lead You
By Dr. Charles F. Stanley

Living Life on Purpose: Discovering God's Best for Your Life
by Lysa TerKeurst

Kingdom Man: Every Man's Destiny, Every Woman's Dream
By Dr. Tony Evans

The Path: Creating Your Mission Statement for Work and Life
By Laurie Beth Jones

IV. TABLE or PLATE: Successful Single Living & Marriage Preparation
Do you want to enjoy being single and be prepared to say "I do" on God's timing?
- *Choosing God's Best* by Dr. Don Raunikar
- *I Kissed Dating Goodbye* by Joshua Harris
- *Table for 1, Please!* by D. Michelle Thompson

V. SPOON: Counseling
a. Chicagoland ABC Counseling – Rev. Watson (Chicago, Illinois)
b. Dr. Dominique Condeveaux, MA, LAC (Denver, Colorado)

ABOUT THE AUTHOR

D. Michelle Thompson is founder of Table for 1 Ministries Inc., a 501(c) 3 non-profit organization birthed out of John 17:21.

"I pray that they all may be One, just as You and I are One."

Regardless of your marital status, every believer should experience greater joy, purpose, and victory. When we end a "me" focus, a powerful "we" emerges in the world at ONE with God. This "we" can start before marriage through loving service to family, friends, and others in work, community, and every part of a purposeful life.

Thompson lives out her own purpose as a marketplace missionary traveling to teach, speak and consult throughout the United States and the Middle East. She remains committed to go wherever God sends her, in 2010, this led Thompson to a two-night speaking engagement for singles at Joel Osteen Ministries.

Current & Upcoming Writing Projects:

Table for 1® Christian Fiction Book Series
Table for 1, Please! (Single Woman's Journey)
Table for One, Thanks! (Single Man's Journey)
Table for One, Still? (TBA) (Married Couples)

Fundraiser for Orphans & Widows
Table for 1, Wholeness Recipes (21-Day Recipes &
Devotional – fundraiser book)

Ministry Curriculum (6-7 Week Lessons)
Table for 1: Purpose
Table for 1: Communication
Table for 1: Accountability

www.ingramcontent.com/pod-product-compliance
Lightning Source LLC
Chambersburg PA
CBHW030258200626
46816CB00002BA/694